Blaze of Glory

Ben Crawford was one of the best lawmen in the business, and when a man named Kane offered him a hundred bucks a month to keep the peace in the fresh, raw town he'd just founded, it sounded exactly like the challenge he'd been looking for. So he took the job ... and spent the next twelve years just waiting for something to happen. It never did.

In fact, life in Kane's Crossing, New Mexico, grew so damn' quiet that the townsfolk eventually decided they didn't really need a lawman at all. But fate had other ideas, because all hell was destined to break loose on Ben's last day in the office. The only question now was, would an older, slower Ben survive it all, or go out in a blaze of glory?

Blaze of Glory

GLENN LOCKWOOD

A Black Horse Western

ROBERT HALE · LONDON

© David Whitehead 2001
First published in Great Britain 2001

ISBN 0 7090 6993 6

Robert Hale Limited
Clerkenwell House
Clerkenwell Green
London EC1R 0HT

Typeset by
Derek Doyle & Associates, Liverpool.
Printed and bound in Great Britain by
Antony Rowe Limited, Wiltshire.

*For a fistful of reasons
that only she will ever understand,
this book is dedicated to my wife, Janet*

ONE

Ben Crawford came awake with a sudden, restless twitch, his heart beating so fast he thought he might well throw up.

When he didn't, he cracked one bleary eye at his gloomy surroundings and set about gathering his wits instead. At first he thought he was still at the office, that something had come up to make him sleep over in the single communal cell. But no: he was at home, he was in bed and, judging by the almost imperceptible lightening of the dark New Mexican sky beyond the open window, he was just in time to witness the start of a new day.

His last, he remembered bleakly.

Still, that wasn't what had jarred him awake. No. There'd been something else: a bad dream, maybe . . . but if it really had been a nightmare, he was damned if he could remember the specifics of it now.

Then he heard it again: a sound like something rooting around in the backyard.

With a determined tightening of weathered lips,

he threw a quick glance at the woman beside him. The steady rise and fall of the Indian quilt told him she was still asleep, and he was glad to see it, for neither of them slept well these days, and hadn't, not since—

But he didn't want to think about that, not now and, if possible, not ever. It was enough just to acknowledge that they were poor sleepers, he and Nora: that Ben himself always slept his best and deepest just before dawn – and that something, or some*one*, had just roused him from his slumber. Someone who had no right to be fumbling around his property.

He threw back the quilt and swung long legs over the edge of the feather mattress, a lean-flanked man with broad shoulders and a paunch that was just beginning to strain at the buttons of his red wool long johns; and as he pushed stiffly to his feet, he felt every one of his five-and-fifty years.

At last, standing tall, he moved down to the mahogany footboard, from the near-side post of which he always hung his gunbelt, and from the embossed, double-loop holster he slid an old, reliable Whitney Navy .36. Firming his grip on the weapon, he threw another look at Nora, satisfied himself that she was still sleeping soundly, then left the room.

They'd lived in the same single-storey, flat-roofed adobe house ever since they'd come to town twelve years earlier, and because the layout of the place had since become so familiar to Ben, he was able to cross the grey hallway and ghost on through the parlour towards the kitchen without the need to actually see where he was going. Around him, the house hissed with silence, only the irregular, runaway ticking of Nora's cheap little shelf clock daring to break the early-morning hush.

He was halfway across the parlour when he heard it again: a muffled, splintery, creaking sound, the kind of creak his ageing backyard fence would make if someone tried to scale it; and, his arthritic joints having loosened up at last, he started moving faster, the polished plank floor striking cold against the soles of his bare feet, until he reached the kitchen.

The back door, he noted with a start, stood ajar.

That brought him up sharp, and sent a sudden, hot flare of anger through him. Until then, he'd assumed that their visitor was nothing more both- ersome than a curious fox, a muskrat or, at a pinch, maybe a brown bear. But now, realizing it was none of the above, he crossed the room with new urgency, moving quickly, softly, with surprising grace.

When he reached the back door he yanked it wide and stepped out into the new day with the Whitney's long barrel jabbing ahead of him. The yard – a track- marked square of red hardpan enclosed by a gappy, peeling wooden fence about six feet high – was empty. Leastways, that was how it *looked* in the poor-but-improving light. But Ben was an old hand at this game. He knew better than to take such things for granted. So he just planted himself there beside the door and used eyes that were no longer bleary but fiercely, sharply blue, to rake the yard, inch by inch, foot by foot.

The necessary ... a tumble-down, open-sided shed cluttered with garbage he'd always meant to clear out and throw away ... the water-pump, its handle set high ... the hen-house. ...

At last he crossed to the necessary, the hardpan feeling cold and scratchy underfoot. He wrenched the loose-hinged door open, saw at once that the one-holer was empty, and let go a long-held breath. A moment later he confirmed that the open-sided shed was similarly unoccupied. He'd gone all right, whoever it was who'd been here. There was nowhere else for him to hide. But who was he, and what had he wanted?

Easing down the Whitney's hammer and allowing the weapon to drop to his side, he headed for the flimsy plank door that was set into the back fence. As he approached it, his eyes dropped to the latch. It was, he thought, old and rusty, just like himself. Whoever their early-morning visitor had been, he'd likely scaled the fence rather than risk forcing the latch and waking him or Nora with the warning screech it was sure to give out.

Ben himself wasn't quite so picky. He lifted the latch – it made a flaky, *skritching* kind of sound – and opened the door. Away to the far north, beyond flatlands stippled with juniper shrubs and, behind them, a jumble of low-growing piñon pines, rose a rugged range of blue mountains. Again he treated the country around and ahead of him to that same slow, thorough scrutiny. Again he satisfied himself that their visitor was long gone.

He turned and went back inside, closed the gate, forced the rusty latch back into place, and was just about to head back to the house when he noticed something he'd missed before: the wood-and-wire door of the hen-house was very slightly ajar.

With a frown, he crossed the yard, dropped carefully to a crouch and peered inside. The hens were strutting around the enclosed space, big-eyed, stiff-necked and clearly agitated.

Ben frowned, made a swift head-count and came up one hen short.

Was that what this was all about, then? Someone stealing hens? As he closed the hen-house door and straightened back up, the frown stayed where it was. He thought, *My last day as town marshal and someone decides to steal from me?* It sounded so ridiculous that he shook his head in dismissal.

But maybe that was how it was meant to sound. Maybe it was someone's idea of a practical joke, stealing from the lawman the minute they took his badge away from him. If that was the case, he didn't think it was very funny.

He suddenly realized that dawn was breaking fast now, the red sun lifting ever higher in what appeared to be a series of rapid oscillations to bleach away the star-picked blue-black of night, and here he was, the marshal of Kane's Crossing, wearing only his combinations. He reached up with his free hand and scrubbed tiredly at his face, then finger-combed his short, fine, white-blond hair. Finally, he sighed again and went back into the house.

As he closed the back door behind him, he made a mental note to pick up a better lock and a couple of bolts. He'd always been aware of just how flimsy the back door was, he'd just never gotten around to doing anything about it. After today, though, he reckoned he'd have all the time in the world to put a few things to rights.

It was then, just as he was about to start over to the Pennsylvania-built chunk stove and boil coffee, that he saw it: something else he'd missed in the pre-dawn darkness.

His missing hen.

It sat in the middle of the scrubbed pine table, a pile of ruffled brown and white feathers from which protruded two stiff, scaly yellow feet ... and whoever had placed it there had snapped its neck first, so that now it stared up at Ben Crawford from out of a head it wore back-to-front.

For a long moment he just stared at the bird, wondering who had killed it and why they'd stuck it on his kitchen table.

If they'd meant it to give him a turn, they'd sure as hell succeeded.

But Ben had never been a man to scare easy, and certainly not for long. Feeling the anger rise in him again, he set the Whitney aside, crossed to the table and scooped up the dead fowl. Beneath its feathers, the flesh was still warm to the touch.

He thought, in genuine bewilderment, What in the hell. . . ?

' 'Morning, Ben.'

He turned with another start as Nora wheeled herself into the brightening kitchen, still clad in her neck-to-ankle nightdress, her pale, heart-shaped face still slightly puffed from sleep. As the wicker chair beneath her rolled to a halt on the other side of the table, she frowned up at the bird in his hands and said, 'What've you got there?'

Not wanting to spook her with the truth, he thought fast and said, 'Supper.' When she made no reply to that, he added lamely, 'Had me a hankerin' for, ah, chicken, see.'

Nora pulled herself closer, the iron-rimmed wheels of her chair turning with a slow creak he had learned to hate, and for one heavy moment he was absolutely certain she knew he was lying. But then she said, 'Well, you'd better hope that one doesn't spoil. In case you've forgotten, we're eating *out* this evening.'

He offered her a blank stare, his thoughts still elsewhere.

'The picnic,' she reminded him.

'Oh, that. Yeah. I . . . I forgot.'

'Well, I hadn't,' she replied mildly. 'Today's a big day, Ben. The day the town honours you.'

'The day the town kicks me *out*, you mean.'

'Now, you *know* that's not true.'

'Well, what else would you call it?'

Nora studied him with humour making her well-spaced hazel eyes sparkle and dance. 'I don't *care* what you call it. All I know is that you won't hear any complaints from me. I'm looking forward to having you home for a change.'

'You'll sing a different tune when I start gettin' under your feet,' he muttered absently, still looking at the hen.

'Oh, Ben . . .' she half-whispered and as she shook her head at him, her expression softened. She was a fine-looking woman with a small, straight nose and a wide, determined mouth, and though she was of an age with Ben, her hair was still as darkly brunette as it had always been, aside from the faintest hint of silver at the temples. 'Ben,' she said again. 'You might know all there is to being a marshal, but you don't know the first thing about what it's like to be a marshal's wife.'

'I should hope *not*.'

'I'm being serious.'

He snorted. 'Way you talk, anyone'd think the job was dangerous.'

'And the way *you* talk, you sound almost sorry that it's not.'

He made no reply to that, but they both knew that he *was* sorry: sorry he'd ever come to Kane's Crossing and allowed himself to grow old here, waiting for a challenge that had never materialized.

'You're up early, anyway,' she said, changing the subject.

'Don't want to be late for my last day on the job,' he replied sourly, finally setting the chicken down.

'Guess I'm jus' so all-fired excited about that gold watch Conrad Kane's fixin' to give me, I couldn't sleep.'

Knowing how he felt about the town council's decision, she made no move to pursue that particular line of conversation. 'Well, you go get yourself dressed,' she offered. 'I'll fix coffee.'

He waited until she started wheeling herself around the table, then took up the revolver and padded back into the bedroom, sorry that he'd acted the way he had. What the hell did he have to feel so sore about, anyway? He didn't have to spend each day looking up at the world from a creaky wicker invalid chair.

Still, this was the day he'd been dreading: his last one in office.

Twelve years earlier, when Conrad Kane had sought him out and offered him a hundred bucks a month to come and keep the peace in the town he'd just founded, he'd done so because Ben Crawford was one of the best and most experienced lawmen in the business. Ben, then in his prime, was the man who'd tamed Bakerville, Gemstone Creek, Hailey Point and half-a-dozen hell-towns just like them.

Conrad Kane had wanted him to do the same for Kane's Crossing.

Kane was a dapper man of slight build, with a deceptively young, almost cherubic face, good teeth and the ready smile of a born politician. He'd come south-west from Jefferson City, Missouri, to start a new town in the wild New Mexico Territory, and he'd convinced thirty other families to make the 700-mile trek with him. In all it had taken them well over a year, but having finally reached their destination, and found land that was to their liking, they'd set to work raising houses and stores, many of them in the hope that the railroad would eventually push south and west and bring prosperity with it.

The railroad – three of them, in fact – had come, all right, but they hadn't come anywhere near Kane's Crossing. Still, Kane himself had chosen his spot well, for the town sat just west of the Goodnight-Loving Trail, and as the townsfolk soon discovered, cattle money spent just as well as railroad money.

That, then, was the job: to keep the lid on a busy cow-town, and organize and maintain some kind of citizens' militia against the Mescalero Apaches who regularly jumped the reservation in order to come a-stealing.

'We've a hell of a town, Mr Crawford,' Kane had told Ben enthusiastically. 'It's hard to imagine that we could better it, but we could. We could attract all kinds of good people to live and work in Kane's Crossing, if they knew we had a man of your calibre keeping the streets safe for them.'

He always had been a flatterer, had Kane. That was the politician in him. But that aside, Kane's Crossing had sounded as if it might just be the new challenge Ben had been looking for: a fresh, raw town that needed bringing into line. And with his work there in Prenticeburg, Texas, all but finished. . . .

By the time they said their goodbyes, the deal had been agreed.

There was just one problem: it hadn't turned out to be much of a challenge after all.

Much as they liked to let off a little steam, the cowboys had, by and large, been a pretty well-behaved bunch. And with the army cracking down on the Mescaleros every chance it got, there'd been no need to form a citizens' militia. Aside from one major incident, life in Kane's Crossing had proved to be so damn' civilized that, eventually, a man like Ben Crawford was considered lucky to have a job at all.

By the time Ben had realized as much for himself, however, it was too late. The last dozen years had taken their toll, and now he felt old, heavy, slow and arthritic. No one else would hire Ben Crawford now. Ben Crawford had become a man with no place else to go, and nothing else to offer: a man who'd wasted the sundown years of his life waiting for a challenge that never came.

Then, one day about six weeks earlier, Conrad Kane had asked him to attend a meeting of the town council.

The atmosphere in the big room above Macy's Saloon had been decidedly uneasy when Ben arrived, and the uneasiness quickly communicated itself to Ben, too. There was a little perfunctory small-talk, an offer of coffee, a couple of councillors asking after Nora, and then Kane drew in a deep breath and got down to cases.

They needed to make economies, he said. And things were so peaceable around town that, after careful consideration, he didn't really see how the town council could justify employing even a part-time lawman, let alone a full-time one.

'I'm sorry, Ben,' he said formally. 'I'm afraid we're going to have to let you go.'

A moment of absolute silence had followed the pronouncement, and it had taken Ben a long few minutes more before he could word a response. All right, he allowed, things had been quiet. He'd give them no argument about that. But they shouldn't take anything for granted. It was a big territory out there, and most of it was still wild.

'This isn't a decision we've taken lightly,' said Tom Sutherland, who ran the Western Union office further up the street. 'We know we still need protection, of a sort. But the truth is, we've already *got* it. The Territory's organized now. We have representation in Congress—'

'I'm not talkin' about politics, Sutherland, I'm talkin' about the *law*.'

'So am I. You want *law*? Hell, man, what with county sheriffs, under-sheriffs and deputy sheriffs, we've got law coming out of our ears! Besides which. . . .' And this was where the room fell deathly quiet, and all the fine citizens who served on the town council started shuffling their feet and glancing guiltily at each other.

'Go on,' prodded Ben, stonily.

'Times have changed, Marshal,' said Fred Harvey,

who managed the Kane's Crossing branch of the Territorial Bank. Tall and big-bellied, he was Kane's staunchest ally in town, a regal-looking man with iron-grey hair, long, wispy sideburns and a frail pair of gold-framed spectacles that were forever clamped to the bridge of his sun-reddened nose. 'A few years ago, a man with your reputation was considered to be an advantage to a town like this. Now he's. . . .'

'He's what?'

'He's a liability,' Harvey said more firmly. 'Now, don't give me that look, Marshal, I don't mean that as disrespectfully as it sounds, and you know it. But let's lay our cards on the table, here. The future of any town is always dependant upon its inhabitants, and Kane's Crossing is no different. To survive, we need to attract the right kind of people. But I'm afraid that the kind of people we'd like to see come and settle here, well . . . frankly, Marshal, I don't think they'd want to live in a town where a man like Ben Crawford keeps the law.'

'*What?*'

'You have yourself a reputation, Ben,' said Kane. 'Oh, it's a fine one, I'm not saying otherwise. But a lot of folks, outsiders, they just naturally assume that, if a town needs Ben Crawford to keep the peace, it must have problems.'

'It's nothing personal, Ben,' stable-owner Mike O'Driscoll said uncomfortably. 'We'll see to it that you're well looked after. There'll be a nice little pension for you and Nora, and we'd consider it a real privilege if you'd stay on here as honoured citizens.'

'You jus' don't want me to wear the badge for you no more,' Ben murmured softly.

O'Driscoll shook his head.

Well, Ben couldn't say he hadn't been expecting it. The way things had turned out, it was bound to happen one day. And, if he was honest about it, it wasn't much of a job to lose, anyway.

Trouble was, though, it was the only damn' job he had.

The town was coming to life by the time he made his way down through the residential district towards his office on First Street, and it was shaping up to be a warm, blue-sky day filled with butterflies, bird-song and, in the middle distance, the rhythmic clatter of busy men wielding hammers. But even now he could hardly believe that this really was it, his last day as a lawman. Maybe that was why the town council had given him six weeks' notice, just so's he could get used to the idea.

Too bad it hadn't worked.

That aside, the business of the dead chicken was still troubling him. Had it just been a stupid practical joke, or something more? Instinct told him it was the latter. But what? Trying to answer that little question had helped to sour what he'd already known would be a pretty sour morning. In fact, he'd been so busy pondering the significance of the dead hen – if indeed there *was* any significance to it – that he'd cut himself twice while shaving: and though he'd continued trying to puzzle it all out as he dressed in the same burgundy-red bib shirt and grey California pants he'd always favoured, he didn't believe he'd come any closer to reaching a satisfactory solution now than when he started.

In the kitchen, he'd eaten his breakfast eggs more to please Nora than to satisfy any particular hunger, and after that a glance at the shelf clock had told him that it was time to leave. Rising, he buckled on his .36 and reached for his old, roll-brimmed black Stetson – and then, impulsively, he bent and kissed Nora roughly on one cheek.

He could still see her face in his mind now, that expression of pleased surprise as she said, 'What was that for?'

The uncharacteristic show of affection had surprised him, too, and Ben's reply was a self-conscious little shrug. 'No reason. Jus'. . . .' But then, unable to find the words that would tell her just what she really meant to him, and not fully understanding himself why his thoughts had suddenly started running along such sentimental, almost morbid lines, he offered her another shrug, and a gruff, 'Nothin'. See you later.'

Now, as the shadow-grey side-alley he'd been following opened out on to First Street, all thoughts of Nora were abruptly curtailed by the sight that awaited him.

First Street – a broad, tree-lined dirt thoroughfare bordered by two rows of detached, whitewashed adobe stores and assorted business premises, was positively bustling. Two local men with ladders were hanging red, white and blue bunting from tree to tree, right the way down to the northern boundary of town. Another two were stringing heavy canvas banners from one side of the street to the other.

Ben's markedly blue eyes narrowed as he read the hand-painted legends, and his mouth, which had always lifted slightly to the left to give the impression of a permanent, short-tempered kind of snarl, suddenly clamped hard.

KANE'S CROSSING SALUTES MARSHAL CRAWFORD! HOORAY FOR CRAWFORD DAY!

Neither did it end there. About midway along the street, he spotted half-a-dozen townsmen unloading trestle tables from two Owensboro wagons and stacking them outside Harper's Mercantile. Later this afternoon, he knew that those same tables would be set out along the centre of the street, and the people of Kane's Crossing would come together and gorge themselves on pan dowdies, corn pone and pumpkin pie, then listen attentively while Conrad Kane sang the praises of the man they were just about to get rid of.

And there, a block further up on the other side of the street, a few more locals were sawing wood and hammering uprights and cross-beams together to form the temporary stage upon which Ben would be expected to address them, his newly presented gold watch in hand.

His eyes hooded as he ran them across the structure. Damn' thing looked more like a gallows he'd seen one time at Fort Smith, Arkansas, than anything else.

But its effect upon him was dramatic. All at once he realized the inevitability of what was going to happen today, and the realization of it seemed to punch some of the life out of him and add years to his tanned, faintly Scandinavian features.

Foolishly, he'd spent the last six weeks hoping that something would happen to show the people of Kane's Crossing just how much they needed a town marshal. A nice little bank robbery, maybe, or a bunch of rambunctious cowboys only he could subdue: anything, so long as it would make them say, *We're sorry, Ben, we were wrong, we see that now. And we'd take it right kindly if you'd, ah, stay on, after all?*

But nothing had happened. Nothing was *going* to happen. There wasn't going to be any last-minute reprieve. These tables, the stage, the flapping banners and bunting, they all showed him just how certain his removal from office really was, and he hated them for it.

He glanced around. By sheer coincidence, he had come to a halt beside the modest, flat-roofed adobe building from which Conrad Kane ran his real estate, insurance and loan agency business. *Kane*, he thought bitterly. *I got you to thank for all this, Conrad.*

Hardly knowing what he was still doing in town,

how he was going to fill his last few hours or why he was still bothering to wear his tarnished brass shield, he started crossing over to the sturdy little jailhouse on the other side of the street, and that was when he heard it, in among all the banging and hammering: the flat, deadly slam of a rifle-shot.

His reaction was as immediate as it was instinctive. He threw himself sideways, landed hard behind a nearby trough and, breathing hard, fumbled his .36 from leather. Moments later he came around the side of the trough, his attention fixed on the narrow alleyway directly opposite, which separated Bert Salmon's Meat Market from Dick Laurel's drugstore.

The alleyway was deserted. Or was it? Empty crates and cartons, stacked high, meant that there were plenty of places a man could hide until the chance came to make his second shot.

Still, it sure *looked* empty.

Hauling down a deep breath, Ben started to rise, but his arthritis made that easier to say than do. He grabbed the edge of the trough with his free hand and started pushing to his feet, feeling old again, and vulnerable, and thinking, Jesus, maybe they're kicking you out just in time, old son. But all the while, his eyes remained locked on the alleyway. If the shooter was still down there somewhere, hiding but figuring to have another go and this time make a better job of it, Ben was ready for him.

At last he stood tall again, and with an undeniable challenge in his stance. His eyes fairly burned

into the early-morning shadows on the other side of
the street, but nothing happened: no sound, no
movement, no sudden, racketing rifle-blast.

A minute ticked slowly into the past, and then he
chanced a swift, sideways glance north along First.
Men were still hanging bunting, tightening the
canvas banners to pull out all the creases, busying
themselves around the base of the ugly-looking
stage with hammers, nails and saws.

He looked at the alleyway again and wondered if
he'd imagined the rifle-shot. Surely not. But he'd
been wanting something to happen that would allow
him to keep his job, and he could hardly turn in his
badge if someone had started sneaking around
town, taking pot-shots at people.

He came around the trough and strode quickly
over to the alleyway, the revolver still fixed tight in
his hand, the man himself ready to react to the first
sign of trouble. He reached the alley-mouth without
event, went in a little deeper and, after a cautious
moment, satisfied himself that it was indeed empty.
Finally, he leathered the .36 and bent double to
examine the ground.

He was looking for a spent shell-casing, something solid that would prove or disprove what had
just happened. Around him, the day grew ten
minutes older, and at the end of it he came up empty.

It pained him to have to admit his mistake. Again
he thought, maybe they're kicking you out just in
time. He walked slowly, soberly, back out into the
glare of First Street, thinking hard, and as his eyes

went back to the front of Conrad Kane's loan agency, he saw it.

A bullet-hole.

It sat high up and a little to the left of the frontage, maybe seven, eight feet up, and eighteen inches or so from the top of the plate-glass window across which Conrad's name and the nature of his business had been painted in flaking gold.

Sight of it made Ben draw up sharp, and he spent the next thirty seconds just looking at the small hole and the spider's-web of cracks the impact had made in the adobe around it.

Suddenly, unaccountably, he found himself thinking about the dead hen again.

This time, the thought made him shiver.

TWO

Not much liking the direction his thoughts were taking, Ben turned on his heel and headed directly for the jailhouse. Unlocking the heavy oak and strap-steel door, he let himself into a cool, shady room with rough, white-painted walls. A big, cluttered desk sat facing him, as did a little black stove with a funnel that ran up the wall and disappeared through the low ceiling. There were two chairs, an old writing bureau (like the desk, overflowing with unfiled paperwork), a sturdy Jenks & Millbush safe in which spare or confiscated weapons and ammunition were kept, and a scratched wooden filing cabinet. A second heavy door, set into the left-hand wall, led through to a modest cell-block that was presently unoccupied.

Ben closed the door behind him and went straight to the filing cabinet, unlocked and pulled open the top drawer – and groaned impatiently when he saw how packed tight it was with out-of-date territorial circulars and dodgers. He didn't have the time for this, he needed information *now*, not this afternoon or tomorrow or quite possibly never at all. Hell, now that he really thought about it, he didn't even know for sure if he *had* the information he was after, anyw—

Hearing the door swing open behind him, he heeled around fast, his right hand dropping away from the dog-eared papers to graze against the butt of the Whitney as a compact man of average height let himself inside.

'Big day today, Ben,' said Conrad Kane, closing the door behind him.

Moving his hand away from the revolver, Ben offered a vague shrug. A particularly nasty notion had occurred to him out there on the street; it had started his heart racing unpleasantly, and he didn't have time for socializing right now. He said, 'Haven't given it much thought.'

Coming deeper into the office, Kane took off his muley hat and glanced around. He was dressed immaculately in a well-cut pale-grey suit, brocade vest and deep red cravat. 'Now,' he said good-humouredly, 'I don't believe that.'

The years had been kind to him, far kinder than they had to Ben. Kane still had that cherubic look to him, that same pleasant, easy smile. His dark-hazel eyes were as sharp and direct as ever, his nose straight, with flared nostrils, his teeth white and even. Though the oiled hair above his ears and at the back of his head was as thick and black as it had always been, however, he was completely, almost shockingly, bald on top. He'd lost the hair quite early in life.

'*Believe* it,' Ben told him, turning back to the filing cabinet. 'Now, if you'll excuse me. . . .'

He hadn't had much to do with Kane since the council meeting. Where was the point? He'd given Kane a wide berth, and Kane, sensing his hostility, had kept his distance. Now, however, Kane frowned and said, with what sounded like genuine concern, 'Everything all right, Ben?'

'Sure.'

'You seem a little . . . agitated.'

For a moment Ben considered telling him all about the hen and the gunshot, but he wanted to make sure of his facts first. 'Busy, is all,' he said after a moment.

Kane chuckled. 'Busy be damned! Put your feet up for a change, let someone else do all the worrying. After today, you're a free man.'

'Sure. But that's *after* today; *today* I still got work to do.'

'Ben,' Kane said more firmly, 'take your beak out of that filing cabinet for a moment.' He waited until Ben had turned back to him, then said softly, 'I know you think you've been treated unfairly, that we've behaved irresponsibly in deciding to do away with your job, but it wasn't just a simple case of economics. We both know just how much you've had to scratch around over the years, to keep yourself occupied.'

Ben hooked a thumb at the filing cabinet. 'You

sayin' I'm scratchin' around to keep myself occupied *now*?'

'I'm saying this is a day of celebration. This is the day we recognize everything you've done for us over the years. I'm saying it's *over*, Ben. You've earned yourself a good retirement, and we plan to see that's what you get.'

Ben pulled a face. 'I really am busy, Conrad. Was there a reason you stopped by?'

'Matter of fact, there is,' Kane replied equably. 'You know I'll be singing your praises at the picnic this afternoon—'

'Jus' before you give me that gold watch, yeah. I can hardly wait.'

Ignoring the sarcasm, Kane went on, 'Well, I wanted to have a private moment with you now, just the two of us, to thank you for, well, *everything*, I guess. Kane's Crossing wouldn't have been half the town it is today if you hadn't come to keep the law here.'

'But now I've served my purpose, it's time to get rid of me, huh?'

'That's not the way I'd have put it.'

'It's the way Fred Harvey put it, more or less. And I don't remember anyone hurryin' to correct him.'

Kane's smile grew a little strained. 'I'm not going to argue the point, Ben. You'll just have to take my word for it. If there was any way we could have avoided this, we would have. But there wasn't. So—'

'So you give me a gold watch and half my salary

as a pension, and that's it. You save the town fifty bucks a month and get yourself re-elected to mayor next spring.'

Kane stiffened, like he'd been slapped. 'I'm sorry you feel the way you do, Ben. You might not believe it, but I have tremendous respect for you. I've always considered you to be a friend, a good friend, and I like to think that you could say the same for me. I'd like to think that we're *still* friends.' Abruptly he stuck out his right hand. 'What say we forget our differences, huh?'

For a long, heavy moment Ben looked at the hand, and then he growled, 'Like I said, Conrad: I'm busy right now.'

As he turned back to the filing cabinet, he heard the quick, angry intake of Kane's breath, heard him turn, cross to the door and let himself out, and when the door slammed shut behind him, he sagged a bit and told himself there'd been no need to be quite so frosty. Hell, Kane was *right*. They *did* go back a long way together. They had always been friends. And, face it, he *had* been forced to scratch around in order to keep himself busy. But there was no sense in agonizing over it. Right now he had more important matters to occupy him.

He dumped a stack of papers on his desk and went through them as quickly as his limited amount of book-learning would allow, but at the end of half an hour he was no closer to settling the matter that was plaguing him. In the end he threw the paperwork back into the cabinet, pinched at the tired flesh between his eyes and then decided to come at it from a different direction.

He grabbed his hat, pulled it down good and tight atop his fine, white-blond hair and went back out onto the street. His belly clenched tight as he crossed to the opposite plankwalk and headed north, up to Mike O'Driscoll's livery stable, but the morning was growing older now, there were more folks about, and he didn't think the unseen marksman would make another try for him quite so soon.

He frowned at the word he'd just used. *Marksman.* Whoever he was, the sonofabitch couldn't have been much of a shot if he'd missed such a clear target by such a wide margin. Unless, of course, that had been his intention: to give Ben a turn, much as he had with the dead hen.

But he stopped that line of thought right where it was. It was taking an awful lot for granted: that the shooting and the dead hen were connected, for one thing, that the marksman had missed him deliberately and not by accident, for another. He knew he couldn't really start drawing conclusions until he had some facts to back them up.

O'Driscoll's livery stable, a long, tall clapboard structure with a pitched shingle roof, was the only place in town that wasn't built out of fat adobe bricks. It took him longer than usual to reach it because of the number of well-wishers who insisted on stopping him and shaking his hand. At length, however, Ben went in through the high double doors and found O'Driscoll himself raking old hay out of empty box-stalls with a long-handled pitchfork.

O'Driscoll was a tall, thin, dark-haired man some-where in his middle thirties, with a pencil neck and a restless Adam's apple, who favoured denim cover-alls and a collarless, striped shirt with the sleeves folded well back from his deceptively slim forearms. When he turned and saw Ben, his sweaty, clean-shaven face broke into an uneasy grin, for O'Driscoll was another one Ben hadn't had much to do with since the council meeting.

' 'Morning, Ben. Looking well.'

Ignoring that, Ben said, 'Come for my horse.'

'I'll saddle him,' said O'Driscoll, eager to please. As he loped down the central aisle to the corral out back, he remarked over one shoulder, 'Didn't think you'd be straying far from town today. You know, what with it being "Crawford Day" an' all.'

'Got some business to attend,' Ben replied vaguely. He watched O'Driscoll catch up his horse, an ageing claybank gelding called Chip, and lead the animal inside. O'Driscoll then took Ben's ancient Federal saddle and blanket from the saddle-tree in the far left-hand corner and set about readying the horse for travel.

While he worked, Ben glanced around. He noticed a chestnut stallion occupying one of the box-stalls down toward the back of the stable and gestured to it. 'Don't believe I've seen that critter around town before.'

'No. He's new. Arrived early this morning.'

'Who fetched him in?'

'Couldn't say.'

'What does that mean?'

'It means whoever rode him in came in early this morning, before I got here. He off-saddled, threw his saddle in the corner, put the animal in the stall you see him in now, and pushed a dollar bill on to that nail you see sticking out there for the purpose.' He glanced in Ben's direction. 'It's not important, is it?'

Ben said, 'Naw,' but he felt a sudden quickening of interest in the horse and its mysterious owner, who had arrived in town earlier that morning, just before his own problems had started.

'There you go, Marshal,' said O'Driscoll at last. 'Hope you have a nice ride.'

Ben took the reins, gathered them up and, fisting one hand around the the horn and the other over the cantle, set about mounting up. But again, his arthritis made the intention easier than the deed, and noting his obvious difficulty, O'Driscoll said helpfully, 'Give you a hand, there?'

Without waiting for a reply, he bent, put a shoulder under Ben's backside and shoved. Ben was boosted into the saddle, where he settled himself with as much dignity as he could manage. After a moment he said, gruffly, 'Obliged, Mike. 'Seein' you.'

He walked Chip out onto the street, then heeled him up to an easy run, grateful that no townsfolk had been around to witness the helping hand and, as the town fell behind them, he told himself again that, if things kept going the way they were, then Kane and his cronies were getting rid of him just in time.

The truth of the statement cut him like a Barlow knife, but he forced himself to face it: he was old now, slow, washed-up, or leastways that's how he felt. And this town didn't have any need for an old, slow, washed-up lawman any more. Damn' town was so quiet it didn't need any kind of lawman at *all*.

Dusty, boulder-strewn short-grass flats, speckled here and there with catclaw, garambullo and saguaro cactus, opened out ahead of him. As he rode north, he kept a wary eye on his surroundings, but though the land looked empty enough, he still had the feeling he was being watched every step of the way.

About an hour later he came across a small herd of grazing Texas longhorns that were still a long way from maturity, each one branded Circle P, he drew rein momentarily in order to check his back-trail yet again. The beeves watched him with idle indifference until, finding nothing to the south, he kicked Chip back to a canter. Then they lumbered awkwardly out of his path.

Thirty minutes later he reached his destination, two long, low adobe dwellings, a barn and a slat-sided corral that were known collectively as the Parsons place.

The Parsons place, he saw at once, had fallen into considerable disrepair since his last visit and, as he walked the claybank into the garbage-strewn yard, he ran his eyes over the main house and remembered the way things used to be. In happier times, Elmer Parsons had run a tight little outfit here.

Now, Circle P was hardly any kind of outfit at all. One by one, all the hired hands had quit or been fired, and pretty soon after that the rot had really set in. Cracked or broken windows had been boarded up, not replaced. Weeds had grown tall alongside the covered porch just left of the house, and poked through gaps in the weathered planks. The corral was falling apart, and more garbage was piled high to one side of the barn. Nearer at hand, a wheel-less chuck wagon sat up on blocks beside what had once been a bunkhouse. By the looks of its threadbare canvas cover, it had sat there for quite a while.

It was just about then that a gunshot tore through the mid-morning silence, and dirt exploded directly ahead of Chip's forehooves.

The horse immediately reared, side-stepped and then started shying backwards, and Ben, reacting instinctively, quickly tightened rein to bring the animal under control as he dragged the Whitney from leather.

'Hold your fire, in there!' he yelled, aiming the order at the distinctive octagonal barrel of Elmer Parsons' old Brown Manufacturing breech-loader, which was projecting from an unglazed and unboarded window beside the front door. 'This is the law, dammit!'

As the echo of the shot rolled off into the distance, Chip reluctantly settled into a taut, bunch-muscled stance, ready to go again at the slightest provocation. Up in the saddle, Ben kept a careful watch on the rifle barrel, also ready to react to whichever course of action Parsons decided to take.

For a time nothing happened one way or the other. Then a husky voice called from the darkness beyond the window, 'That you, Ben Crawford?'

'It's me, Elmer.'

'You alone?'

'Uh-huh.'

There was another moment's hesitation. Ben hardly dared draw breath. Then, finally, the rifle barrel lowered and was withdrawn.

Ben's broad shoulders dropped a notch and he shoved the Whitney away just as the front door opened and a gangly, bare-headed, underfed man in loose coveralls and a stained undervest came out onto the porch, his long, slim breech-loader held slantwise across his narrow chest. The man, Elmer Parsons, squinted at him and said, 'You all right, Marshal?'

'I ain't *bleedin'*, if that's what you mean.'

'Lucky for you my damn' eyesight's gettin' worse by the day.'

He came out into the sunshine, and Ben saw his long, sunburnt, whiskery face, with its rheumy blue eyes, long nose and rubbery lips, more clearly. Although he was careful not to show it, he was shocked at just how dramatically Parsons, who was somewhere in his fifties, had aged. But neglect had done that for him, Ben reminded himself: neglect, guilt and a deep, all-consuming sadness he had never been able to conquer.

'Mind if I light an' set a spell?' asked Ben, when no such invitation came from the other man.

Parsons said unenthusiastically, 'Sure,' but his troublesome eyes were scanning the land behind and to either side of his visitor while he spoke.

With a wince, Ben swung down, led Chip towards the house and tied up loosely at the tumbledown hitch-rack. 'Kinda jumpy this mornin', ain't you, Elmer?' he remarked casually.

Parsons reached up with one hand and scratched energetically at his shaggy grey-black hair. 'Man gets that way, I guess, iffen he lives too long on his own.'

He turned and shuffled back into the house, and Ben went after him, into a gloomy keeping room, or parlour, that was crammed with big, heavy slabs of black walnut furniture: a Boston rocker that had been Esther Parsons' favourite, a cluttered table with matching ladderback chairs, a sofa that was worn shiny and split open, and some dust-coated whatnots. The room smelled stale, of long-settled dust and the lard-oil Elmer burned in his lamps, and it was dark and airless, like a blocked mine-shaft. The only attempt at decoration that Ben could see was an almanac calendar that had been pinned to the wall above the cold stone fireplace.

'Well,' said Parsons, stopping in the centre of the room and turning to face Ben, 'what is it brings you out here, Marshal?'

Ben said one word. 'Jared.'

Even though Parsons must have known it was coming, the name still caught him like a kidney-punch. He flinched at the sound it made, but then recovered himself and said tonelessly, 'Don't b'lieve I know anyone of that name.'

Ben looked him right in the face and growled, 'The hell with your eyesight, Elmer. It's your memory you should be worried about, iffen you can't even remember your own son.'

'I don't *have* any son,' Parsons replied doggedly.

'Pretendin' he don't exist don't make it so, much as we'd like it to,' Ben said with a shrug. He brushed past the other man and went to the fireplace, where he asked, suddenly, 'What's the occasion?'

Parsons had turned on his heel to watch where he went. Now he said uncertainly, 'I don't, ah, follow you.'

Ben indicated the almanac calendar with a jerk of the thumb. 'You've circled the sixteenth. That was two weeks ago las' Tuesday. What was the occasion, Elmer? Birthday?'

The other man shook his head irritably. 'I disremember. Some such foolishness, I daresay.'

But Ben was pretty certain he'd already worked it out for himself, and, if he was right, it was the answer he'd come here to get, the confirmation he'd been dreading. 'He's out, isn't he?' he said softly. 'That's his release date you've marked there.'

'I don't know what—'

'The hell you don't!' Ben snarled. 'You've been *expectin'* him, haven't you? That's why you threw a shot at me jus' now – you thought I was him, comin' home.'

'I think you better get out of here, Marshal!' blustered Parsons. 'I already told you, I don't know no Jared!'

For a moment Ben's anger flared quick and fiery inside him, but almost immediately it died and before he knew it, all he felt was sympathy for the tall, thin wreck of a man who stood before him. 'Aw, Elmer,' he said heavily. 'Elmer. . . .'

For a while, Parsons didn't trust himself to look anywhere but at the unswept puncheon floor, and then, when he finally spoke, his voice was so low that Ben had to strain hard to hear what he said.

'I've tried to not to think about him for years,' he half-whispered, and there was something cracked and wretched in his tone. 'It's been easier that way, to pretend he jus' didn't exist. An' it worked, for a while. But then, it's like you wake up one mornin', an' all of a sudden six years've gone by, an' he's out again.' He swallowed, shook his head, went on in a rush, 'I couldn't see why he'd want to come back here. They's nothin' here for him, not now, an' he knows it. But I guess I allus kinda dreaded that he would, for the devilment of it if nothin' else. So, you're right about that, too, Marshal: I *have* been expectin' him.' Suddenly he looked up, and his eyes were big and sharp in his tortured face. 'Whyfore you come out here to see me, anyway? W-what's happened?'

'I don't know myself, yet,' Ben confessed. 'Just a couple things that made me think of Jared.'

'Well, if he shows up here, I'll kill him myself,'

Parsons said thickly, and his voice had a kind of suppressed sob in it. 'Y-you know, it's a hell of a thing for a father to say about his son, but they should'a hung him when they had the chance. I wish they had. Was the best thing they *could'a* done with him.'

Silently, Ben agreed. Jared Parsons had never been easy to like, not even as a boy. He'd always had a quick, cruel temper to him, just as he'd always carried a chip on his shoulder because a leg broken in childhood had mended badly and left him with a lumbering kind of shuffle for a walk. He'd been a loner, had Jared, a bully-boy when Elmer finally sent him to the Kane's Crossing Elementary School, and a spoilt little brat at home. But Esther Parsons, God rest her, had doted on her only child. Whatever her little Jared wanted, her little Jared *got*.

And the lonely, embittered boy had wanted plenty. A dog. Rabbits. A long-limbed colt. But as they found out later, he hadn't wanted any of them for company.

After a couple of weeks, the dog had drowned – apparently by accident. And one night a few weeks after that, the rabbits just vanished, leaving only a smear of blood on the ground behind the barn, where Elmer had knocked up a crude kind of hutch for them. Later, and entirely by chance, Elmer found the bodies in a shallow grave about a hundred yards to the south.

Though he never raised the matter with Jared himself, and never mentioned it to Esther, each furry little body had been stabbed right through the heart.

The truth of the boy's sick nature suddenly became obvious, and from that moment forward, Elmer kept a careful watch on him. But Jared seemed to sense as much, because there was no further trouble. The colt survived Jared's dreadful need to kill, though even that poor creature didn't escape entirely unscathed, for Jared wasn't shy when it came to using his big Spanish colonial spurs on its tender flanks, or the cruel spade bit that eventually tore the inside of its mouth to mincemeat.

Still, for all his faults, Jared kept pretty much to himself, so Elmer decided to turn a blind eye and hope he'd eventually grow out of whatever it was that ailed him. But as he grew older, the boy started to develop an interest in girls, and one girl in particular: young Katy Barrett, who worked as a waitress down at the Allen Cafe. Jared spent months trying to spark Katy, but, perhaps sensing for herself that there was something in him that wasn't quite *right*, she rebuffed his advances.

That was a bad mistake, because Jared didn't take kindly to rejection.

As if to prove it, he rode into Kane's Crossing one dark night six years earlier, with one single, terrible purpose in mind: to teach Katy Barrett a lesson. He found himself a nice little spot in the shadows directly opposite the eatery and spent the evening watching her serve at table, and at closing time he followed her as she made her tired way back to the home she shared with her parents. Somewhere along the way he closed the distance between them, jumped her and tried to rape her. She fought back as best she could, scratching him and kicking, but he took everything she had to give.

It was only when she started to scream that he panicked.

Ben never could decide whether or not murder had been a part of it all along, but that was certainly the way it ended up. Katy started screaming, something in Jared snapped, and next thing, the sonofabitch had fastened his hands around her throat and strangled her with such force that he snapped her neck and left her like a – and here, the significance of it struck Ben for the first time – like a fresh-killed hen.

Ben himself, making a routine patrol of town at the time, had heard that single, muffled scream and come upon the scene just before Jared could light out. There'd been a chase through darkened back alleys, but it hadn't been much of one because of Jared's disability; and then Ben had brought him down, cuffed him senseless and taken him in.

The murder left the people of Kane's Crossing in a kind of daze. After all, it was the only real trouble they'd ever known. Katy's parents never did get over it, and moved on shortly afterward. Out at Circle P, meanwhile, Esther Parsons took the news just as bad. Unable or unwilling to believe that her precious son could have killed the girl, she retreated into herself. She wouldn't speak, she wouldn't eat, she wouldn't sleep. She just sat in her rocker and wept.

Come to that, Elmer, too, had a hard time trying

to come to terms with what had happened. Had he spoken up sooner, had he tried to get the boy some kind of help for the sickness inside him—

But he hadn't. He'd ignored it, in the desperate hope that ignoring it would make it go away.

There was more to it than that, of course, a lot more, but all at once Ben didn't want to think about any of that, for just as Elmer had been forced to live with the guilt of it ever since, so too had Ben himself, and his was a terrible guilt indeed. Yeah, he thought sourly. Jared should've hanged. And but for Ben, he *would've*.

If only he hadn't interfered. . . .

Suddenly he heard a strange, gurgling sound, and realized with a start that Parsons was crying. He muttered awkwardly, 'Don't take on, Elmer. What's done is done. If Jared's got any sense, he'll never show himself in this bailiwick again.'

'Iffen he had any sense,' the other man countered wetly, 'he'd never have killed that girl in the first place.'

There was nothing Ben could say to that, so he clapped the rancher gently on the shoulder and went back to the door. *En route* he said, 'I jus' remembered. This is my last day in office. They're retirin' me today.'

Sleeving his nose, Parsons said without much real interest, 'Y-you don't say.'

'Yep. They're givin' me some kind of a gold-watch-an'-speech send-off later. I'd appreciate to see you there.'

'Aw, I don't—'

'You been stuck out here for too long,' Ben countered. 'Do you good to get away from this place for a while. An' I know for a fact that Nora'd like to see you again.'

Parsons looked surprised. 'Nora? Huh – now that I *don't* believe.'

'You should,' said Ben. 'That's the thing about Nora, see. She ain't like you an' me, Elmer. Got no bitterness in her at all.'

Parsons digested that, then murmured, 'I . . . I'll think on it.'

'You do that. Then you smarten your damn' self up an' get your skinny backside into town, you hear me? You an' me, we've known good times an' bad, Elmer, an' though I ain't made up my mind yet which way today's gonna end up, I do know this much: I want you there to see me off.'

THREE

As Ben rode away from the Parsons place, that thought whispered through his mind again.

If only I hadn't interfered . . .

But he had. He was a lawman, it was his job to interfere, if another man looked like breaking that law. So that's what he'd done.

But at what cost?

He shifted irritably in his saddle, still unwilling to think about the rest of it. Even six years on, the consequences of his one big moment as marshal of Kane's Crossing still hurt to remember. But as Chip continued to carry him back to town, the memories came whether he wanted them to or not. There was simply no stopping them.

As he had already noted, Katy Barrett's murder had left the town in a state of shock. Katy had been well-liked, her parents well-respected members of the community. Most townsfolk felt the girl's loss almost as keenly as her people did themselves. It was as if they, too, had been somehow savaged by what had happened, and when you're hurting like that, the natural impulse is to strike back and hurt the thing that's hurt you.

The people of Kane's Crossing were no different.

Immediately following his arrest of Jared Parsons, Ben had wired the territorial capital to request that a circuit rider come and try the case at the earliest opportunity, but Santa Fe had replied that there would be a delay. Apparently, Judge Shuyler was presiding over another matter up in Holbrook just then, and wouldn't be able to get there for another four, five weeks minimum.

That, he told himself, was where it had really started. If they could've tried Jared there and then, if the people could only have seen justice done within a matter of days instead of weeks, that would have been an end to it. But with feelings running so high around town, no one was in much of a mood to wait.

The thing came to a head about five, six days after the murder. It was early evening, and Ben was standing in the open office doorway, enjoying the gradual easing of the day's oven heat, when he suddenly grew aware of a peculiar heaviness to the air, as if something momentous were about to happen.

With a frown he glanced north, along First Street. The tree-lined thoroughfare was strangely deserted, and darkening fast but for whatever lights had started showing at store windows.

In the same moment he heard the sounds of

raised voices coming from Macy's Saloon, and knew for sure that trouble was on the way.

He turned, went back into the office and across to the chunky safe. Quickly, but not hurriedly, he worked the tumbler, turned the brass handle, hauled open the thick, heavy door and reached inside.

He took out a long, hammerless Colt shotgun, broke it open and stuffed one shot-filled pin-fire cartridge into each barrel. Then he snapped the weapon shut again and went back to the door, the Colt cradled like a baby in his folded arms.

He waited like that for maybe twenty minutes, until the batwing doors down at Macy's suddenly shoved outward and a line of liquored-up townsmen poured out in a flood. Ben could still see their flushed faces in his mind: Bob Tolliver, Saul Collins, Art Pitcher, Ed Graham and a good twenty more besides, all of them mad enough to spit rust as they hurried along the middle of the street in a determined knot. He could still see their elongated shadows, leaping and bobbing from store-front to store-front, still hear the low, ominous rumble they made as they talked to each other about teaching that murdering bastard a lesson he'd never forget.

Tom Sutherland was in the lead. He was the one holding the rope, and Ben remembered being surprised about that because Sutherland, a stocky thirty-year-old with pale, freckly skin and a wide, fair-bearded face, was just about the last man he'd have ever associated with a lynch-mob. Sutherland, the Western Union man, had fierce political aspirations. He served on the town council, loved the power it afforded him, and was seriously considering running against Conrad Kane in the forthcoming mayoral elections.

For another stretched moment he watched them come closer, and then he strode out across the plankwalk and down into the street to meet them head on and, as he went, he raised the shotgun and fired one barrel into the cooling night sky.

The roar it made, coming right out of the blue like that, stopped Sutherland and all the others in their tracks – which, of course, was precisely the intention. Ben kept walking, the shotgun held crosswise over his chest now, smoke from the right-side barrel wisping and drifting back over his left shoulder like the departing ghost of a just-dead snake.

Slowly, the echo of the single shot faded and died, leaving a heavy, oppressive silence in its wake. No one moved; no one spoke. There were one or two nervous throat-clearings, but that was all.

'All right,' called Ben, and he sounded more impatient than angry, 'that's far enough! I can see what it is you fellers got planned, but it's not gonna happen, not now, not ever. So you jus' break it up there and go on home, you hear me?'

Tom Sutherland glanced around at his companions, then back at Ben. 'We're coming through, Marshal,' he said. 'We've decided. To hell with the courts. That sonofabuck's gonna hang right here, tonight!'

'That sonofabuck's gonna hang, right enough,' Ben agreed. 'But when they string him up, it'll be done legal. Iffen I step aside an' let you men do the job now, well, that's murder.'

'Murder, hell!' said Sutherland, and when the men clustered behind him started yelling their support, Ben was no longer surprised to find the Western Union man there. There were votes to be had at this little shindig, he realized. It was a chance for Sutherland to show himself as a man of the people. 'Stand aside, Ben,' Sutherland said imperiously. 'No need for you to get involved in this.'

'I'm *already* involved,' Ben replied gravely. 'Now, back down, Sutherland, an' you other fellers, too. There'll be no lynchin' here while I keep the law, you hear me?'

'Stand aside, I said,' repeated Sutherland, grinding the words out between clenched teeth, and suddenly he lurched forward and made a clumsy grab for Ben's arm.

Ben, seeing it coming, shook the other man's weak, pen-pusher's grip loose and stepped in close, and because these stupid, half-drunk men needed something to shock them back to their senses, he rammed the butt of the shotgun hard into Sutherland's belly, and Sutherland grunted, sagged and went down on to his knees. Another man – the normally placid Ed Graham, who clerked at the Territorial Bank and was known to be backing Sutherland's selection for mayor – tried to rush him, but Ben quickly turned the shotgun around and clipped him a short, telling blow on the jaw. Graham went back, hit the dirt on his shoulder-blades and started moaning groggily.

Before anyone else could try their luck, Ben backed up a few paces and braced the butt of the shotgun against his hip so that its snout could pin every man-jack of them right where he was. *'Break it up. I said!'* he yelled, and now he was furious, because he hadn't wanted it to come to violence. 'I'm not tellin' you again! Now, turn around an' take your wounded with you, an' we'll forget this foolishness ever happened! If not, well, all right. Come ahead, an' start dyin'.'

That heavy, oppressive silence descended again. Men stared at him; men glared at him, but no one spoke a word.

'Well?' he demanded roughly.

He looked from face to face, and such was the rage in him now that he had a hard time trying to get any man there to meet his eyes. Yeah, he thought, they were hurting, and they wanted to do something to ease the pain. They'd thought that taking Jared Parsons out and hanging him was it, but now they knew different.

Bob Tolliver bent and helped Sutherland to his feet. The Western Union man looked sick and wet-eyed. His tone moderating, Ben said, 'You'll thank me for this in the mornin', Sutherland,' but Sutherland only showed him a bitter sneer.

'The hell you say!' he snarled.

'Me, I reckon you're right,' allowed Art Pitcher,

clearly shaken. 'It's a hell of a thing to take a man's life, ain't it, Marshal? I mean, even a low-life skunk like Jared Parsons?'

Ben nodded, watched them pick Ed Graham up off the street and disperse.

Back in the jailhouse, he unloaded the shotgun, pulled it through to keep the barrels nice and clean, then locked it back in the safe. He should have felt pleased with himself. He'd upheld the law and stopped the locals from doing something they'd likely regret to the end of their days, but all he felt was a peculiar sense of loss. Rough-housing that way with Sutherland and Graham . . . he shouldn't have allowed the confrontation to go that far. And though Art Pitcher had seen the sense of his argument, he had a feeling that Sutherland, Graham and their cronies would never forget the way he, Ben, had treated them this night.

He boiled coffee and poured himself a cup. While that was cooling, he poured another for his prisoner and took it through to the cell-block, which was a cheerless room about fifteen feet square, lit now by the greasy amber glow of a single peg-lamp. A wall of bars split the room in two, so that it comprised a narrow aisle and one modest communal cell. Jared Parsons, he saw, was curled up on a bunk against the far wall, his legs jack-knifed up against his chest, his head buried beneath folded arms.

Ben looked at him for a moment, then said, 'Coffee's up.'

A muffled voice said, 'Keep it.'

Ben shrugged easily. 'I will.'

He turned to go, but stopped when the muffled voice said, 'Wait.'

Jared Parsons unfolded himself slowly, turned and rolled up off the bunk. He was tall and lean, just like his father, and though he had a gaunt, half-starved look to him, his arms were sinewy and muscular, and there was power in his unusually large, long-fingered hands, more than enough to crush and snap the neck of a young girl. He looked like a scarecrow right then, because he'd lived and slept in the same plaid shirt and grey California pants for nearly a week, and his long, blue-black hair was all mussed up.

He shuffled across the floor, his left leg twisted at a crazy angle, and wrapped his vein-threaded fists around the bars, and Ben, looking at him, saw a long, spiteful face much, much older than its twenty-one years, with deepset eyes as blue as Elmer's but nowhere near as kindly, high, pronounced cheekbones that shoved at a pocked, sun-darkened skin as if they wanted to get out, and a long, thin nose that was more like the beak of a buzzard than anything else.

'Di'n't have the guts, did they?' he said after a moment. His grin revealed small, uneven yellow teeth, and a tongue that came out to wet his thin, sneery lips at regular intervals. 'They thought they did. But when it come to it, they di'n't have the sand.'

Ben knew he was referring to Tom Sutherland and the other townsmen. 'They had the sand, all right,' he replied. 'They jus' realized you wasn't worth the effort.' He held out the mug in his left hand. 'Here.'

Jared took it and blew through the bars to spill steam off the surface of the brew. `You think you stopped 'em, don't you, Marshal?' he asked. 'You di'n't. They jus' wanted to make it *look* like you stopped 'em, so they could go home an' tell their women what they tried to do to make the streets safer for 'em.'

'Sure,' said Ben, feeling too tired to argue about it. 'Whatever you say.'

'Don't you believe me?'

'I don't really care one way or the other. In any case, whatever time I bought you here tonight, it's only temporary. You'll hang for what you did, Jared, but it won't be some kinda half-assed mob affair where you take twenty minutes to choke yourself blue. It'll be orderly, by the book. One drop, one snap, an' that's that.'

Jared glared at him. 'I won't hang,' he said, and the confidence with which he said it made Ben's skin crawl.

Not that he let it show. 'You jus' keep tellin' yourself that,' he replied after a pause. 'But don't for one minute make the mistake of actually *believin'* it.'

Jared shrugged and let go a long, heavy sigh. 'Well,' he said, 'for what it's worth, I thank you for what you jus' did out there.'

Surprised by the expression of gratitude, Ben said, 'Ferget—'

But that was as far as he got.

In the next moment, Jared flung the contents of the mug at him; they caught him full in the face, and while his eyes were screwed shut, while the burn of the coffee was scalding all other considerations from his mind, Jared reached through the bars, grabbed him by the front of his bib-shirt and hauled him forward.

Ben smashed against the bars with a dull clang, and Jared let him stagger back about a foot, then pulled at him again, so that he hit them a second time. He did that twice more in quick succession, and while Ben was still disorientated, bleeding from a cut on the forehead and another under one eye, he tore the key-ring from Ben's gunbelt.

Ben, his eyes still streaming from the sting of the coffee, felt himself flung backwards like a discarded toy. He hit the far wall, slumped and shook his head in a desperate attempt to clear it. He heard a jangle of keys, a fumbling scrape of metal on metal and thrust clumsily back to his feet, already knowing he was too late—

Jared, flinging the cell-door open, came out like a twister and kicked him in the belly. Ben grunted, fell back again, tried to curl up and make himself small before Jared could kick him some more.

It didn't really help much.

For the next half-minute he took a merciless beating that disorientated him still further. For thirty agonizing seconds, Jared was absolutely uncontrollable in his desire to hurt and keep on hurting.

Then, at last, the rain of blows tapered off, and Ben sensed Jared close by, felt his quick, raspy breathing against his skin. Jared reached down, tore the .36 from his holster and pistol-whipped him clumsily across the back of the head.

Thunder, then. No, not thunder, *footsteps*. The sonofabitch was getting away!

Ben started clawing his way up the wall, cursing himself, cursing Jared, grunting with the pain of it and forcing himself to ignore all his many hurts in his determination not to let the bastard get away.

He stumbled back into the office, no more than three, four feet behind his limping prisoner, made a wild, drunken kind of lurch, grabbed Jared and swung him around. He saw Jared's face clearly, then – it was flushed and sweaty, just like the faces of the men who'd been so set on hanging him a short lifetime before – but most of all he noticed Jared's eyes. They were big and crazy, and they glowed like they were lit from within.

Jared swung the Whitney at him. The barrel opened a slice in his face but did no more damage than that. He made another lunge at the killer, and it was then that the law-office door swung open.

The sound it made, a sharp creak, distracted both men, and Jared, shoving Ben away from him, wheeled around to face this new obstacle to his freedom.

All he saw was a target.

All Ben saw was his wife.

He remembered yelling, '*Nooooo!*'

But Jared was already bringing the gun up, the weapon was already booming, bucking, spitting flame, and in the next moment Nora jerked and slammed backwards, the covered tray she'd been carrying slipping from her grasp to land with a crash of china at her feet.

Like a man in a dream, Ben watched her fall sideways to the floor and screamed it again: '*Nooooo!*' Jared, meanwhile, seized the moment and ran for the door. He caught his shoulder against the frame as he leapt over Nora and the impact jarred the Whitney from his grasp. The weapon hit the floor with a heavy *clunk*, and then he was gone. Ben heard his boots clattering against the plankwalk, but couldn't tear his eyes away from Nora. Nora, stretched out in a growing pool of blood. . . .

Shaking like a man in a fever, muttering nonsense to himself, he crawled over to her, certain she was dead, and gathered her up in his arms, the pain in him so bad he felt that he might explode with it. To hell with Jared: Nora was all that mattered right now.

And then she gave a spastic little twitch, made a rough, coughing kind of sound, and somewhere deep inside him he realized that she was still alive. He started yelling for help, anyone, and pretty soon after that, Doc Warren shoved him aside and got busy right there on the floor, saving the life of the woman who meant everything to him, and more.

God, he thought, what a night that had been. Even now he remembered how slowly the seconds had passed. Every minute had seemed more like an hour. Every hour had seemed more like a week. But eventually the star-picked sky outside had started to lighten with false dawn, and finally the long night was over, and Doc Warren, looking hollow-eyed and stubbly, had done as much as he could.

'The bullet shattered her pelvis, Ben,' he explained gently, as they stood side by side over the unconscious woman. They'd moved Nora into the cellblock following Doc's initial examination, and that was where the medic had done all his probing, slicing and stitching. Now he made a quick gesture with one finger. 'Then it turned and kept going until it lodged right here, at the base of her vertebral column.'

'You got it, though?' said Ben.

'Sure I got it,' Doc replied. 'But it wasn't easy. It chewed her up, Ben. There was a lot of damage. A *hell* of a lot.'

A swallow, a lick of dry lips. 'Wh-what're you sayin', Doc?'

'I'm saying she'll live . . . but she won't ever walk again.'

The news had struck him like a blow. He remembered some sort of moan slipping from his lips. *Nora, Nora. . . .* And that was when the guilt set in, because if only he'd let Sutherland and the rest of them have their way, if only he'd let them take Jared out and hang him, none of this would've happened.

But. . . .

But he was the marshal of Kane's Crossing.

And, God help him, he'd had to interfere.

Back in the present, he reined down, so shaken by the memories he'd just relived that he didn't trust himself to ride on right away. He unhooked his canteen, unstoppered it, took a pull, rinsed his mouth and spat. His hands were trembling and he felt cold, even though the day itself was hot.

He swung down and poured water into his up-turned hat for Chip, and while the horse drank, he let the story play itself out to the bitter end.

Nora had pulled through, just like Doc said she would, and if there had been tears – as he knew full-well there had – then she had shed them in private. Not once in all the years since it happened had he ever heard her complain about her lot. He'd often wished that she would. But he had come to learn that Nora was bigger than that.

The same couldn't be said for Esther Parsons, though. For her, what Jared had done to Nora had been the final straw. She'd seemed to lose the will altogether after that, and passed away six weeks later.

About a month after her funeral, a United States marshal spotted Jared up in Raton – it was that weird mixture of shuffle and limp that gave him away – and collared the bastard right there and then. He stood trial and Ben testified against him, and if there'd been any real justice, Jared would've hanged. But he hadn't. Because there had been some doubts as to his sanity, the judge had given him six years in New Mexico's Harding County Penitentiary instead, and as he now knew, that term had come to an end just over two weeks earlier.

Jared, he told himself again, was back in circulation.

All at once he felt strangely drained, really tired beyond imagination. Not only that, but suddenly he felt anxious too, to see Nora again. Remounting, he settled himself slowly, carefully, then rode on.

He was almost within sight of town when he spotted three riders up ahead, travelling in the same direction. They were riding gaunted horses line abreast, and they slouched in their well-worn saddles like men who'd come a far piece and wanted only to get where they were going.

Grateful for the distraction they would provide, Ben kicked Chip up to speed, and when they heard him coming, the three men shortened rein and hipped around to watch his approach. When he was near enough, they all exchanged nods.

' 'Mornin', Marshal,' offered the man in the middle. He, like the others, was dressed in creased, alkali-coated rangewear. He was about thirty, with a full, blond steerhorn moustache and a lean, not unpleasant face that was shaded by the wide brim of a high-crowned brown hat. As he touched his tobacco-stained fingers to the brim, his smile brought deep creases to the nostrils of his slightly hooked nose, and made his full mouth peel back to show off surprisingly good teeth.

' 'Mornin',' Ben replied. As he said it, he gave them what appeared to be a brief, casual glance that was actually nothing of the sort. He saw that one was forking a sorrel mare, the second a dun with a brown mane and tail, the third a grey-sprinkled roan. He saw that two of them – the speaker and the younger man to his right – shared the same grey, almond-shaped eyes that marked them as kin, most likely brothers. And he saw that the first man wore a short-barrelled Peacemaker, the second a Merwin & Hulbert Army .44, the third a Smith & Wesson Russian of the same calibre, with a big, six-and-one-half-inch rounded barrel.

'You boys headed for Kane's Crossin'?' he asked.

'That we are,' said the man with the blond moustache. He gestured to the shield on Ben's shirt. 'You be the local law?'

'Uh-huh. Crawford.'

The other man took the hint and introduced himself. 'John Elliott,' he said, reaching over to offer his hand. 'My friends call me Johnny. This here's my kid brother Matthew, an' my cousin, Patch Samuels.'

'Glad to know you,' said Ben.

Matthew Elliott, he saw, was about five years younger than his brother, and of a slighter, more average build. In his snug-fitting Kentucky jeans and waist-length corduroy jacket, Johnny Elliott struck him as a pretty capable specimen. Matthew, by contrast, was about five or six inches shorter, with a paler, rounder, frecklier face and longer, slightly blonder hair.

It was hard to put an age to their cousin, this Samuels. Ben figured that he was older than Matthew but younger than Johnny. Fine black hair spilled from beneath his battered sugarloaf sombrero to curl over the narrow collar of his dark-blue shirt. It framed a tired, weathered face with a thin black beard. He was puffing on a small corncob pipe, making regular little clicking sounds with his lips as he drew on the stem, and it took no stretch of the imagination to see why they called him Patch: he wore a frayed black patch over his left eye, and the sun-pink skin above and below it was ploughed with old scars.

'What brings you boys to town?' Ben asked, as they all started pushing forward again at a companionable walk.

'Lookin' for a man named Parker,' said Johnny Elliott. 'Says he's got a job for us.'

'Cattle job?'

'Uh-huh.'

'Well, I hope you got your facts straight. No ranchers name of Parker in these parts.'

'Oh, he's not from around here,' explained Matt. He wore a brown leather vest over a collarless boiled shirt, riveted Levi pants and spur-hung Justin boots. 'He jus' said for us to meet him in Kane's Crossin'.'

'Well, I wish you boys luck with it.'

'Thanks.'

Another ten minutes brought them to the outskirts of town, where Ben's three companions got

their first look at all that red, white and blue
bunting, the trestle tables and the rough-and-ready
platform that looked more like a gallows. From the
edge of his vision, Ben saw Johnny Elliott lean
forward a little and squint at the gaudy canvas
banners that were strung across First Street. 'What
be the purpose of all this finery, Marshal?' he asked
after a moment.

'It's my last day on the job,' Ben replied grudgingly.

'You movin' on?'

'Retirin'.'

'Well, it sure looks like they plan to do you proud,'
opined Samuels, speaking around the stem of his
corncob pipe.

Matt agreed. 'Buy you a drink, Marshal?' he
asked. 'To wish you well?'

'I 'preciate the offer,' Ben replied, 'but I got things
to do.'

'Fair enough.'

With a nod, Ben drew rein outside the stable and
swung down, watching as his recent companions
angled their mounts across towards Macy's. Nice
fellers, he thought. But as he watched them
dismount and tie up outside the saloon, he felt his
mood darken again. Today they were fixing to start
a job. Tomorrow he was going to be out of one. And
as if that wasn't bad enough, he still had Jared
Parsons out there someplace, just a-sneaking
around the woodpile.

He sensed rather than heard someone coming up

behind him, and turned just as Mike O'Driscoll reached out to take Chip's reins from his grasp. 'Here,' said the stable-man, still a mite leery of him. 'I'll turn him out for you.'

Ben said, 'Thanks.' Then: 'Mike, that stallion in yonder stall. Anyone come back to claim him yet?'

'Not so far.'

'All right.'

He started off up the street, figuring to drop in on Nora before he made his way back to the office, but he hadn't gone more than a dozen yards before he heard hurried bootfalls clattering against the plankwalk behind him. A moment later urgent fingers plucked at his shirtsleeve and he hauled up, heeled around and came face to face with a short, chunky man dressed in the charcoal-grey vest and pants of a well-tailored three-piece suit.

'Marshal, Marshal . . .' gasped the man, clearly winded by his exertions. 'Thank goodness you're back! When Mr O'Driscoll said you'd left town on business—'

Already jumpy, Ben said, 'All right, Frank, all right. What's the problem?'

The chunky man clung to his arm while his harsh breathing calmed. His name was Frank Landis, and he owned and ran one of the town's two hotels. Somewhere in his late fifties, he had brittle, crinkly grey hair and a darker pencil moustache that appeared to balance on his pursed upper lip like a trained worm. Bleak by nature, he always seemed to be worried about something – but this time he

looked as if he might just have good cause. Glancing
to left and right, he leaned a little closer and, lower-
ing his voice, said, 'I've got a man in one of my
rooms, Marshal. He only checked in this morning.'

'And?'

'And he's *dying!*' hissed Landis, as if he couldn't
believe it. *'Dying!'*

Ben threw a frown across the street, toward
Landis's solid-looking two-storey hotel. He thought
about Jared, about the stallion someone had stabled
up at Mike's place at first light, about the man
Landis believed to be dying, and wondered if there
was a connection between them. 'You'd better fetch
Doc,' he murmured.

But the other man only shook his head. 'You don't
understand,' he whispered urgently. 'This man, he's
not *sick*, Marshal, he's *bleeding*.'

Ben's eyes narrowed. *'What?'*

'I think . . .' said Landis, a little desperately, 'I
think he's been shot!'

FOUR

Ben turned Landis around, put a hand between his shoulder-blades and started propelling him back across the street. 'I think you better tell me everything,' he said.

'There isn't much to tell,' Landis replied, as they closed on the hotel. 'He came in a little after dawn, said he wanted a room.'

'What did he look like?'

'Tall, wide shoulders – a redhead, I think. About forty.'

Ben frowned. It wasn't Jared, then. 'Go on.'

'Well, I thought from the first that he was sort of . . . *careful* when he moved, as if he were favouring himself. But I just figured he'd been on the trail a while and was tired. You know, saddle-stiff.'

'I know. Did he give you a name?'

'He signed the register as Douglas, first initial G, from Wyoming. Didn't have much else to say for himself, just paid a week in advance, took his key and went upstairs. I didn't really think much more

about him until I came around the desk a couple of
hours later and, uh, saw blood on the carpet.'

'*Much* blood?'

'Enough that you wouldn't want to lose it,' Landis
replied queasily, his dark-brown eyes going wide at
the memory. 'There was a . . . a trail leading across
to the staircase. I followed it right up to the door of
his room.'

'Did you knock, see if he was all right?'

'No, I did *not*!' the hotelier replied indignantly. 'I
came to fetch you, but your office was empty.'

He made it sound like an accusation, and Ben
thought, with an evil kind of relish, *You just wait,
Frank. Starting tomorrow, it'll be empty twenty-four
hours a day*.

'What made you think he'd been shot?' he asked.

Landis shrugged and blew air in a defeated sigh.
'Shot, stabbed, where's the difference? It's how he
came by his wounds in the first place that matters,
isn't it?' His mouth thinned to a grimace. 'I don't
mind telling you, Marshal, I'm at the end of my rope.
I mean, supposing he dies in that room, a man who's
been shot? An outlaw, perhaps? What's that going to
do for business?'

'All right, Frank, no need to take on. We'll get it all
straightened out.'

They entered the hotel lobby. The white adobe
walls were panelled to about half their height in
dark, polished wood, and a few coloured prints in
gilt frames, and potted plants standing on waist-
high plaster columns, gave it a sense of warmth and

welcome. Ben glanced to the left, where a narrow staircase led to the rooms above, then went over to the desk – actually a fairly short counter to the right – where he inspected the register. The last entry confirmed what Landis had already told him. In crabbed, laboured handwriting he just about managed to decipher, *G. Douglas. Casper, Wyo.*

Stepping back, he looked at the carpet underfoot, then back at the staircase. Odd, still-damp patches showed where Landis had scrubbed out the blood-stains. 'What room's he in?' he asked.

'One-o-seven.'

'All right. Let's go.'

They climbed the stairs with Ben in the lead. Around them, the hotel was so quiet it might have been deserted. Reaching the first-floor landing, Ben freed the Whitney from leather, then ghosted on along the narrow hallway, once again exhibiting his peculiar and unexpected sense of grace.

A floorboard creaked underfoot. He broke stride and cursed it. Then he was there, his back to the wall just left of the door marked '107', and Landis was hovering to the right, his face strained, his mouth pursed, his thin moustache clinging for dear life to the sweat-pebbled skin beneath his broad nose.

Ben signed that Landis should do all the talking, then reached across and rapped cautiously on the door. Clearing his throat, Landis called uncertainly, 'M-Mr Douglas? Are you, ah, all right in there?'

Their eyes locked while they waited for a reply.

For a long moment there was only silence. Then, barely audible, a man's voice called back, 'Trying to get some sleep.'

At Ben's urging, Landis said, 'It's just that, ah, I thought you might have . . . injured yourself. Would you like me to call a doctor?'

Another long silence. Then: 'I'd like to *sleep*.'

'All right,' said Landis, placatingly. 'Sorry if I, ah, disturbed you.'

He threw Ben a look that said, *Do you want the pass key?* Ben shook his head. He didn't think he'd have the time to use it, not if he wanted to get the drop on the man on the other side of the door. Instead, he grabbed the brass doorknob with his left hand and rammed the portal with his shoulder.

The door flew in with a splintery wrench and Ben went right in after it with the Whitney pointing the way ahead. The small room was in semi-darkness because Douglas, or whatever the hell his name was, had pulled the thin drapes. For vital seconds, all Ben saw were grey shadows and black shapes: a chest of drawers, a chamber set, a wardrobe, a chair, a bed—

And a man stretched out on the bed.

A man holding a pistol on him.

He came up straight, knowing he had to take command of the situation immediately, and barked, 'All right, Douglas, let's not start bustin' off caps here, iffen we can help it. I reckon we're both too young to die.'

The man on the bed made an odd, wheezing choke

of sound. It took Ben a moment to realize that it was a chuckle. 'I don't think I got too much say in the matter,' he croaked at last.

He let his gun-arm drop back to the mattress, no longer strong enough to support the weight of the ... Ben could just about identify it in the gloom, a Remington Army .44. He put up his own weapon, came a little deeper into the room while Landis hovered nervously in the doorway, and plucked the weapon from Douglas's grasp. Then, stuffing the heavy .44 into his belt, he went to the window and drew back the drapes to let some light and air into the stuffy room. All the while, Douglas watched him through feverish, resigned eyes.

He came back over to the bed. Douglas, he saw, was stretched out on a creased blue eiderdown, his free hand, the fingers stained red, pressed flat to a spot just above his left hip-bone. He was, as Landis had said, tall and brawny, about forty, with a sweat-darkened spill of fair-red hair, a pale, lightly freck-led face that was blotchy and highly coloured now with fever, blue eyes and white-blond eyelashes. His breathing, Ben noted, was hard and irregular.

He reached down and gently lifted the other man's hand away from the wound. A patch of blood about the size of a clenched fist stained Douglas's grey shirt. The blood smelled cold and metallic, but there was something else to it – another, more unpleasant, odour: infection. Without looking around, Ben said, 'Go fetch Doc, Frank. Hurry, now.'

'I 'preciate the thought,' said the man on the bed,

as Landis beat a hasty retreat, 'but I th-think it's too late.'

Ben eased Douglas's shirt open a fraction and saw a puckered, purplish bullet-hole speckled with pus the colour of mustard. 'I've seen worse,' he replied casually. He had, too . . . but not much worse.

He took a handkerchief from his pocket and went over to the chamber set, where he poured water from a flowery jug into a flowery bowl and soaked the square of cloth. He squeezed it out, fetched it back and started wiping Douglas's burning skin. 'You got a name?' he asked. 'A *real* name, I mean.'

The other man licked his lips. He seemed on the verge of sticking with Douglas, but then said in a low, defeated voice, 'What th-the hell does it matter, now? Sure I've got a name. It's McGivern. Alex McGivern.'

'I'm Crawford,' said Ben. 'You wanted by the law, McGivern?'

'N-no.'

'Then how come you're masqueradin' as someone called Douglas? And how'd you come by this here wound?'

'L-long story,' said McGivern.

'We're neither of us goin' anywhere.'

McGivern stared up at the ceiling, trying to bring order to his thoughts, to find the right place to begin. While he was thinking, Ben splashed water into a misty-looking glass and helped him raise his head so that he could drink. McGivern choked a bit as the water went down, but whispered at the end of it, 'Ahhh, that's better.' Then: 'I'm a . . . *was* a P-Pinkerton man,' he husked. 'Quit about f-four months ago. Been on the move ever since.' He gave another of those strange, bitter little chuckles. 'R-running scared, m-more like.'

'What's that supposed to mean?'

'You m-make enemies in this business,' breathed McGivern. 'It was my m-misfortune to make some of th-the worst.'

Ben made an impatient sound between his teeth. 'Quit talkin' in riddles.'

'F-fair enough. Ab-bout six months ago, there was a s-series of train hold-ups up in . . . south-western Kansas. Nasty ones. Rails were lifted, the trains derailed. Lots of . . . injuries, lots of . . . confusion, f-fear. Th-that's when they struck. Gang of m-masked men. Th-they'd work their way through the carriages, lifting money, jewellery, anything that looked as if it might be w-worth stealing. It happened th-three times in all, and in the last robbery a passenger who tried to . . . put up a fight w-was . . . shot dead, and the . . . the conductor was wounded. That's when the Atchison, Topeka and Santa Fe called in the Agency, and I got the assignment.'

'Which was?' said Ben softly.

'To run the robbers to ground,' gasped McGivern. He signed for another drink, and Ben obliged him. 'W-wasn't much to go on,' the wounded man continued afterwards. 'W-we knew there were four of them, but they always wore flour-sack hoods and nev . . . never used names. But the robberies always occurred within a thirty-mile radius of a town called . . . Rawley, so that's where I got started.

'W-went in, posing as a drifter, spent a l-lot of time just . . . loafing, sipping whiskey and buying drinks to see what I could p-pick up in the way of . . . gossip. There was s-some general ill-feeling around town toward a . . . a rancher and his kin who operated a hard-luck spread just outside of town. Figured it might be w-worth checking out, so I took a ride out there, tried to get them to take me on but th-they said they weren't hiring. So I went and found m-myself a hidey-hole instead, and just kept watch on 'em from a distance, to s-see if there was anything to all that talk.

'You're a lawman,' McGivern went on weakly, 'you know what it's like. You hang around, and nothing happens. That's how it was for me, at first. Then, come sun-up one morning, they pulled out, the whole clan. I was asleep, didn't see 'em go, but soon as I realized what'd happened, I saddled up and went after 'em.' His eyes came up to Ben's face. They were big, bloodshot and far-away. 'I didn't see 'em hit the train, but I sure as hell caught 'em leaving the scene.' He swallowed, reliving the memory. 'I guess they thought I had a posse with me, 'cause they turned tail and ran. I . . . I went after them, we exchanged shots, one of 'em grabbed his leg, fell from his saddle.

'I decided to q-quit while I was ahead, swung down and arrested him. Turned out to be that r-rancher, all right.' McGivern offered a tight smile. 'I reckoned that was all th-the evidence I needed, that we could arrest the whole d-damn' family, but . . . no. They went and hired themselves a r-real sm-smart lawyer. The old man was caught dead to rights, wasn't any hope for him, but there was no hard evidence on the rest of them. All I'd seen was three men in flour-sack hoods. C-could've been anyone.'

'So they walked free?'

McGivern nodded tiredly. 'They walked free, b-but there was justice of a sort: they lost their ranch.'

'How so?'

'It didn't matter that we couldn't get a . . . conviction. Everyone knew they were guilty. The local bank decided they'd likely been paying their mortgage with the proceeds of the . . . robberies, and foreclosed.'

'And the man you caught, this rancher?'

'Jury was . . . s-satisfied that he'd been involved in all the robberies, including the one where th-the passenger was . . . shot dead. Judge sentenced him to hang, and he did. But his b-boys swore they'd fix me for . . . for giving evidence against him.'

Ben gestured to McGivern's wound. 'And this is it?'

'Th-they tried once just . . . just after the trial. Tried to back-shoot me from an alleyway one night, but they were too . . . eager, gave themselves . . . away. Couldn't prove it was th-them, of course . . . but the Agency sent me n-north, just to get me out of their way.

'It didn't work. They got wind of it somehow, . . .

picked up my trail, followed me and . . . tried again. I managed to stay ahead of the game, disappeared, but when they found me again, my nerve s-slipped and I decided to call it a day. I quit the Agency, came south-west, made another stab at losing myself, and really thought I'd done it that time. Gave myself a new name, took my beard off. . . .'

His bloodless lips curled. I could've saved . . . myself the . . . trouble. They found me again, ambushed me f-four nights ago: up along . . . Nelson Creek. I took a bullet but m-managed to return . . . fire, chase 'em off before they could come in and . . . finish the job. I lit out, think I lost 'em again, wound up here and figured to either die in bed or rest up a while, get my wound doctored and then push on.'

Ben digested all that, then asked, 'You got anything to back your story, McGivern?'

The other man motioned vaguely towards a set of saddle-bags in the corner. 'I got a letter of reference from the Agency,' he near-whispered. 'That'll prove who I am. If you think it's worth the . . . the effort, you can wire my old line manager in Chicago, if you like. He'll confirm the rest.'

Ben didn't think that would be necessary. He went over to the window and looked down into First Street, trying to figure out what to do next. He spotted Landis almost immediately, leading Doc Warren along the opposite boardwalk, then across the busy thoroughfare. 'How sure are you that you've given these here varmints the slip?' he asked without looking around.

'I've given up being sure about *anything* where those . . . bastards are concerned,' McGivern replied bitterly. 'Anyway, wh-what does it matter, now? I reckon they've just about . . . finished the job this time, don't you?'

'The hell they have,' Ben replied, turning back to him. He heard Landis and Doc clattering through the lobby, climbing the stairs. 'Strikes me you've had a rough time of it, McGivern,' he murmured. 'But you're among friends now.' Suddenly he frowned. 'These here fellers on your trail: what names do they go by? How will I know 'em if I see 'em?'

McGivern swallowed some more, then said, 'Two of 'em're . . . brothers. Blond hair . . . grey eyes, just like their old man. Third one's a cousin, lost an eye in some kind of . . . accident, years back, wears a . . . patch now.'

For the second time that day, Ben felt himself go cold. 'Name of Elliott?' he asked in somebody else's voice. 'Elliott, an' Samuels?'

'You *know* 'em?'

'Know 'em, hell,' Ben replied through set teeth. 'I jus' rode in alongside the bastards not more'n twenty minutes ago.'

While Doc Warren peeled back McGivern's shirt to check for himself the extent and severity of the wound, Ben went downstairs with Landis following anxiously at his heels. 'Who is he, Marshal?' asked the hotelier. 'Is he under arrest?'

Ignoring him, Ben crossed the lobby, went out on

to the plankwalk and squinted down the street toward Macy's. When he spotted the horses of his three recent companions still tied up outside the saloon, his shoulders dropped a notch, because that meant the Elliott boys and Patch Samuels were still busy washing the trail-dust off their tonsils.

'Marshal?' Landis prodded urgently. 'Is he a bank robber? A murderer?'

Still not making any reply, Ben went back up to McGivern's room with Landis dogging him every step of the way. Doc was taking McGivern's pulse when he came through the door. He raised his eyebrows questioningly, but Doc's sidelong glance gave nothing away, so he came right out with it. 'Is he gonna make it?'

Doc shrugged. 'Hard to tell. I've got to get the bullet out, irrigate the wound thoroughly, insert a drain to stop the infection from re-establishing itself—'

'Is that a yes or a no?'

'It's a maybe. With the right treatment and enough rest – *maybe*.'

Ben nodded. 'All right. Can he be moved?'

Doc, looking tall and cadaverous in his black frock coat and grey pants, snorted. 'Which part of the word "rest" didn't you understand, Ben?'

Not bothering to reply, Ben said to McGivern, 'Reckon you could stand a bit more shakin' around, Pinkerton man?'

McGivern gave him a dreamy-eyed look. 'Do I have a choice?'

'Not iffen you want to keep breathin'.'

'Let's . . . get to it, then.'

'Right. Doc, gimme a hand here. Don't worry about your gear, McGivern. I'll come back for it later.'

Doc, however, stayed right where he was. 'What in the name of Caesar's ghost do you think you're playing at, Ben? Move this man now and you'll *kill* him.'

'If I *don't* move him, he'll die for sure,' Ben countered. 'McGivern's a lawman, Doc, an' he's made an enemy or two along the way. Three such're in town, right now, lookin' to finish him off. Hotel's the first place they'll check, once they're through wettin' their whistles down at Macy's, so I figure we'll move him to my place. You can doctor him there an' Nora can nurse him when you're finished.'

While Doc thought about that, Ben turned his attention back to McGivern. 'By the way, a chestnut stallion turned up down at the livery stable this mornin'. Yours?' When McGivern nodded, Ben turned briskly to Landis. 'Frank, get on down to Mike's place an' tell him I said to take the stallion an' lose it, *pronto*.'

Landis frowned. 'Lose it? What do you mean, "lose" it?'

'Cheez – I mean take it someplace where no one else'll find it,' Ben growled irritably. 'An' tell Mike, if anyone but me comes askin' after it, he never saw it, right?'

'R . . . right.'

'Oh, an' Frank. Tear that last page out of your

register and get rid of it. 'G. Douglas from Casper, Wyoming' was never here, you got that? Douglas was never here, *McGivern* was never here, me an' Doc was never here. Anyone comes askin', you don't know a thing.'

Landis nodded and shook his head all at once. 'I don't know a thing,' he breathed nervously.

'Good man. Now get goin'.'

As Landis left the room, Ben and Doc helped McGivern climb slowly to his feet. McGivern gave it his best shot, but by this time he could hardly stand, much less walk, so Ben lifted him carefully into his arms and told Doc to go on ahead and make sure the coast was clear. More by luck than design, they got the wounded man downstairs without mishap, and out through the back door undetected.

Carry-dragging him between them after that, they took the long way around town to Ben's house, deliberately keeping to back alleys and dog-trots to avoid being seen. As far as Ben was concerned, the less people who knew about McGivern, the better. That way, if the Elliott boys and Patch Samuels couldn't find him in town, they'd likely push on and continue their search elsewhere.

But even as he thought it, Ben knew that such a course of action wasn't really the answer to McGivern's problem: it was merely delaying the inevitable. No: a man couldn't run forever, 'specially not from such determined miscreants as these here train-robbers. Sooner or later he had to make a stand and finish it once and for all – or allow someone else to make the stand for him, if he himself wasn't up to it.

By the time they reached Ben's house, the effort of carrying McGivern between them had left Ben and Doc sweaty and breathless. Ben opened the door, called, 'It's only me!' and then he and Doc hauled McGivern straight through to the bedroom. Doc was just checking McGivern's pulse again when Nora wheeled herself out of the parlour, a ball of green wool skewered with knitting needles dumped in her lap.

'Ben?' she asked, sensing more than knowing that something was wrong. 'What—?'

Leaving Doc to get on with it, Ben closed the bedroom door behind him. 'Somethin's come up,' he replied, speaking in a low voice. 'Help me put some water on to boil an' I'll tell you all about it.'

He was as good as his word. While Nora heated a pan of water for Doc to sterilize his surgical irons, he told her all about McGivern and what he was doing there. Nora listened without interruption until he was through, then glanced uneasily toward the back door and said, 'These men . . . are they *very* dangerous?'

'They're jus' kids,' he replied vaguely.

'That's not what I asked,' she reminded him. 'Do you think they'll cause trouble? If they don't find the man they're after, I mean?'

He shrugged. 'I don't know. I'll keep an eye on 'em, anyway, just in case. Meantime, you keep the doors locked, you hear? Keep away from the windows an' don't let anyone in but me or Doc.'

'All right.'

He threw a quick glance at the shelf clock and said, regretfully, 'I better be pushin' along.'

He was almost out the door when she called impulsively, 'Ben.'

He turned to look at her.

'You won't . . .' she began. 'I mean, it's your last day, Ben. You won't do anything . . . silly, will you?'

They both knew what she meant. Having wasted so many tedious years as a small-town marshal, the prospect of locking horns with the men who were after McGivern must surely represent one final chance for him to recapture something of the old days, to go out, as the dime novelists said, in a blaze of glory. Knowing him as she did, she knew also that the temptation to brace these men must be enormous . . . and she wasn't at all sure that he would be able to resist it.

Well, neither was he.

Still, he dredged up a smile and said, 'You worry too much.' And then he was gone.

As he made his way back down to First Street, he thought some more about McGivern. A decent man. But a marked man, too. He thought about Doc, working on him at this very moment with probe, scalpel, clamp and forceps, and of the heady, sweet stink of morphine hanging in the close, bedroom air. And he thought, too, that even if McGivern survived all that, he'd still be a marked man, always moving on, jumping at shadows, checking his back-trail.

It was no kind of life. But if he, Ben, could stop the Elliotts and Patch Samuels right here in Kane's Crossing . . . well, he'd be doing McGivern a hell of a service, and ending his own days as a lawman in fine style.

The thought of mixing it up with McGivern's tormentors stirred an old, all-but-forgotten excitement within him. He could still do it, he *knew* he could. But it stirred something else, too: fear that maybe he *couldn't* do it. He'd never doubted himself before, but now, as he remembered the way Nora had just looked at him, he realized for perhaps the first time just what he stood to lose if he went ahead, all filled with confidence, and found they had the beating of him after all.

He came out on to First Street just as the noon stage from Fort Sumner swayed in from the north, a big bottle-green Concord with bright yellow wheels that kicked up a cloud of dust in their wake. Late again, he thought sourly. Should've called it the one o'clock and had done with it.

As the stage drew to an untidy, harness-jingling halt outside Frank's hotel, he threw another glance down at Macy's and saw that the Elliott and Samuels horses were still standing hipshot at the rack.

He crossed the street, his expression turning thoughtful again. By his reckoning, Patch Samuels and the Elliott boys had been drinking now for the better part of an hour. That was what, two, three beers apiece? Something of the sort. He wondered if two or three beers would be enough to slow them down, make them clumsy – and give him an advantage if he *did* decide to brace them after all.

He let himself into the office, took off his hat and scratched irritably at his fine fair hair. What with one thing and another, it was turning into a hell of a day, and his life was rapidly filling up with problems. He shook his head, hardly able to think straight, and crossed over to the stove, where he set about fixing a cup of coffee he didn't particularly want.

The coffee was just coming to the boil when the door swung open and an inoffensive-looking man in a plain brown suit stepped inside. The face beneath the newcomer's grey derby was thin, weathered and framed by long, curly side-whiskers the colour of sand. Ben had never seen him before, but the small leather case he carried in his left hand pegged him as a drummer of some sort. He'd probably just come in on the stage.

The man returned his appraisal through innocuous hazel eyes that were shielded by a pair of smudged, wire-framed spectacles, and after a moment he said, 'Marshal Crawford? Marshal Ben Crawford?' He was about thirty, Ben thought, and a nervous thirty at that.

Ben nodded. 'I'm Crawford. Help you, Mr. . . ?'

'Jameson,' said the other man, his voice soft and mild. 'Arthur Jameson. And yes, sir, I believe you *can* help me.'

All at once his manner changed, and bringing up

a Remington double derringer he'd been holding down at his right side, he hissed, 'I've come for my money, Marshal. And if you don't pay me what you owe me right this minute, so help me, I'll shoot you where you stand!'

FIVE

Wondering just what in hell this was all about, Ben said carefully, 'I don't think that'd be such a good idea, Jameson. Not least because I don't owe you a red cent.'

Jameson, a compact man of average height, came deeper into the office and heeled the door shut behind him. He was nervous, all right: it showed in every jerky movement he made. 'Don't owe—!' he repeated, and gave a short, hard cackle. 'By God, you've got some nerve, Crawford! You owe me the better part of fifteen hundred dollars, and you'll pay up now or I'll know the reason why!'

Ben exhaled noisily through his nostrils. 'Put that damn' gun down,' he said more firmly. 'I mean it, mister! I get mad as all get-out when people point guns at me for no good reason, so why don't you jus' put it down, an' let's start over?'

Jameson said, 'Oh, no. You don't wheedle out of—'

But by then, Ben was already moving.

He threw himself forward, closed the six or so feet that separated them in a rush and quickly slapped Jameson's gun-hand aside. With his other hand he grabbed Jameson by the lapel and shoved him backwards until his spine slammed hard against the door. A high-pitched cry came out of the man as his derby hat left his head, hit the floor and rolled drunkenly under the desk, and behind his smeared glasses his eyes went wide as Ben brought his free hand back in a tight fist—

But the blow never landed.

Even as he glared at Jameson, now squirming ineffectually in his iron grip, Ben felt his anger dull. Whoever the hell this brown-suited man was, and whatever the hell he thought he was doing here, it was over. One look at the defeat in those eyes, and the down-turned horseshoe of that small, prissy mouth, said it all. Jameson was finished, and he knew it.

That being the case, Ben saw no good reason to hit him. Instead, he tore the derringer from Jameson's fingers and threw it on to his cluttered desk, and as he did so, he ran the man's name through his mind again. *Jameson . . . Jameson. . . .* Now that he came to think on it, it did sound vaguely familiar, even though he knew he'd never seen the man before in his life.

He pushed away from Jameson and went slowly, breathlessly, back to the stove.

'Oh, I bet you're real proud of yourself now, aren't you?' sneered the man in the brown suit, trying to massage some feeling back into the fingers of his gun-hand.

'Mister,' said Ben, 'you wear your welcome out real *quick*, you know that? Now, let's hear it: just how'd I come to owe you all this money?'

'Playing the innocent now, are—'

'Just answer the damn' question.'

Jameson's eyes slid away from Ben's face. 'My uncle died about four months ago,' he replied, a little breathless himself. 'Joshua Wheedon.'

That did it. When Jameson said that name, everything fell into place. For many years, Josh Wheedon had owned and operated a modest little spread about twelve, fifteen miles west of town. He'd been fair and direct, and Ben had liked him a lot, for though he kept mostly to himself, he was always the first man to step forward if he figured his neighbours might need a helping hand. It had been a crying shame when Ben had gone out to Wheedon's place one day about four months earlier, intending to collect taxes on behalf of the US Land Office, only to discover instead that the old man'd taken a tumble, cracked his head on the edge of a table and lain dead for a month, maybe longer.

He said, 'You're the nephew.'

Now it all came back to him, and would've come sooner had he not been so preoccupied with other matters just then. Arthur Jameson. A farmer from someplace up north ... southern Nebraska, he thought, and the only kin Josh Wheedon had. 'You jus' got in?' he asked.

'Uh-uh.'

'Want some coffee?'

'What I want,' grated Jameson, 'is my money.'

'You've already got your damn' money,' snapped Ben. 'In accordance with the powers invested in me by this here shield of office, I arranged an' conducted the sale of Josh's property an' possessions, an' wired you a banker's draft for as much as I was able to raise. I got a record of it around here someplace—'

'Perhaps you have,' allowed Jameson, stiffly. 'But records can be falsified – *Marshal*. And the fact remains that I haven't seen a nickel of that money.'

'Well, why the hell didn't you *wire* me about it? You didn't need to come all this way an' stick a gun in my face.'

'I *did* wire you. I threw good money away on wire after wire, but never received a word in reply. *That's* why I decided to come in person.'

Ben frowned. 'You sure you don't want some coffee?'

'I'd sooner have an explanation,' replied Jameson. 'That, an apology, and the money.'

'Well, you'll get all three, iffen you've truly got 'em comin'.'

'You'll find that I have,' murmured Jameson.

Ben wondered what time it was, figured one-twenty, maybe a little after. Thinking quickly, he said, 'Stow your case in yonder corner, mister. You an' me are gonna do some investigatin'.'

'Can I take my derringer back?' Jameson asked truculently.

Ben snorted. 'What do *you* think?'

He grabbed up his hat, gestured that Jameson should do likewise, then headed for the door.

Outside, banner-strewn First Street was finally starting to quieten down as the day moved inexorably toward its hottest point. Wagon and horseback traffic had thinned considerably, and the boardwalks, too, were taking on a deserted look. As they crossed the street, Jameson asked, 'Where are we going?'

'The bank. Iffen you won't take my word for it, maybe you'll take theirs.'

Now it was Jameson's turn to snort. 'Like I said just now,' he muttered, 'records can be falsified.'

Ben threw him a withering glance. 'By Christ, you don't try all that hard to be liked, do you?'

'Not where money's concerned, no.'

The Territorial Bank was a square adobe block of a place with small, barred windows and sun-bleached green blinds. Fred Harvey's only employee, Ed Graham, was just hanging a *Closed for Lunch* sign on the inside of the half-glass door when they climbed up on to the plankwalk directly in front of it. Recognizing Ben, Graham's sour mouth clamped down hard at the edges, because he'd never forgiven Ben for clipping him on the jaw the night of the lynch-mob.

The smartly attired bank clerk glanced briefly at Jameson, then back at Ben. He had a strange, pale face, with the features all crowded together in the centre, and though his quiet, cultured voice was all but lost behind the glass, his thin lips were easy enough to read. *I'm sorry, Marshal. We're closed.*

Ben nodded. 'Yeah, yeah. But I got some urgent business, Ed.'

Graham flicked another glance at Jameson. He was somewhere in his middle-thirties, with long, dark sideburns, black, centre-parted hair and a button nose. *Can't it wait? We open again at two.*

'Just open 'er up, Ed,' Ben growled impatiently.

Behind the glass, Graham sighed heavily and began to unlock the door. *All right, all right. But Mr Harvey's not going to* 'like this. He's very punctilious about the bank's hours, you know.'

'This won't take long,' said Ben, brushing past the clerk with Jameson following on behind.

It was noticeably cooler inside the bank, because the walls were so thick that most of the harsh New Mexican heat bounced right off them. Ben bellied up to a long counter behind which stood Fred Harvey's private office, a walk-in vault and general working area, the whole screened off from the customers by a tarnished metal grille that extended as far as the low ceiling.

'This is highly irregular, you know,' Graham muttered officiously, taking a turnip watch out of his vest pocket and checking the time just to underline the point.

'Too bad,' said Ben. 'Is Fred around?'

'I'm here, Marshal,' said Fred Harvey.

All eyes turned as the bank manager squeezed his tall, big-bellied frame through his office doorway and rolled ponderously up to the other side of the counter. 'Can I be of assistance?' he asked, looking from Ben to Jameson and back again through the gold-framed spectacles that were forever clamped to the bridge of his sun-reddened nose.

'Think maybe you can,' said Ben. 'This here's Arthur Jameson. Josh Wheedon's nephew.'

Harvey's eyebrows – a deep iron-grey, just like the hair that crowned his regal head – lifted in surprise. 'My dear sir,' he said warmly, 'a pleasure to make your acquaintance. Your uncle was a fine man, and we still feel his loss in and around these parts.'

Jameson started to mutter something in reply, but Ben talked him down. 'Thing is, Fred, Jameson here says the banker's draft I sent him followin' the sale of Josh's property never reached him. Is that possible?'

Harvey didn't even have to think about it. 'If it was sent,' he said, 'it would have got there.'

'Well, it was sent, right enough,' said Ben. I deposited all the money right here an' left the rest of it to you fellers.'

Harvey considered the matter briefly, then said, 'I didn't handle the transaction myself, but we're sure to have a record of it.'

'That's if the transaction *was* made,' pointed out Ed Graham.

Ben fixed him with a scowl. 'What's that supposed to mean?'

The clerk looked a little embarrassed. 'Well, don't take this the wrong way, Marshal, but . . . I myself have no memory of handling such a matter. And if Mr Harvey here didn't handle it. . . .'

'You sayin' I never came an' handed over that cash, Ed?'

Graham looked helplessly at his boss, who said quickly, 'Now, let's not jump to any unpleasant conclusions. I'm sure there's a perfectly reasonable explanation for . . . whatever has occurred. Edward, would you be kind enough to bring out the ledgers for the last. . . ?'

'Four months,' said Ben.

Graham went to a door at the far end of the counter and let himself into the cage on the other side. Impulsively Ben followed him in, Jameson still tagging along behind. They waited while the clerk selected two fat ledgers from a shelf just inside the vault, and then he and Fred Harvey went to work, poring over page after page of crabbed, handwritten entries that formed a record of all the bank's trans-actions for the past sixteen weeks.

At length both manager and clerk straightened up and exchanged a brief glance that Ben caught and didn't like the look of. Then Fred Harvey turned to Ben and Jameson and said, 'I'm sorry, Marshal. There doesn't seem to be any record of the transac-tion to which you refer.'

'Then you'd better check the records again, Fred. I fetched that money in here, as near as dammit fifteen hundred dollars, took my receipt an' left it to you fellers to send the draft on to Jameson.'

'What can I say?' asked Harvey, spreading his

hands. 'Of course we'll check again, but we don't usually make mistakes, Marshal, especially not when dealing with such a large sum.'

Jameson suddenly piped up, 'Do *you* have an account with the bank, Marshal?'

Ben's eyes narrowed. 'What the hell's that got to do with it?'

'I was just wondering if you didn't deposit my uncle's money in your own account,' Jameson replied bluntly. 'By *accident*, of course.'

Struggling to hold down his temper, Ben said, 'Check it, Fred.'

'Wait a moment,' said Graham. 'If you could produce this receipt you say we gave you, Marshal. . . .'

Ben glanced at him and nodded. 'Sure. I got it over at the office someplace.'

'Well, go fetch it, man,' urged Harvey, anxious to settle the matter once and for all.

'Yes,' added Graham. 'That receipt's all the proof you need.'

Ben, just about to turn away, suddenly froze and looked back at the clerk with a strange expression on his face. It could have been his imagination – there was a good chance that it was – but something about the way Graham had said what he had made it sound like he already knew that Ben would never find that receipt, not because it didn't exist, but because it was no longer anywhere for the finding.

Unnerved by the look, Graham squirmed a bit and said, 'Is there . . . is there a problem, Marshal?'

Something else, something that Jameson had mentioned earlier, suddenly fell into place, or leastways Ben thought it did. 'These receipts you issue,' he said, his voice dropping lower. 'Each one carries a number, right?'

'Yes,' said Fred Harvey.

'And the counterfoil, the bit you keep, that carries the same number.'

'Of course.'

'Then I got a better idea,' he breathed. 'You go through your little book o' counterfoils, Ed. I got me a feelin' you might jus' find one missin'.'

'What?' asked Harvey.

Ben said, with sudden, absolute certainty, '*You* took that money, didn't you, Ed?'

Stiffening at the accusation, Fred Harvey said warningly, 'Have a care, Marshal. That's a serious accusation, and unless you have proof—'

Ignoring him, still looking at Graham, Ben curled his lip. 'By Christ, I guess I made it easy for you, didn't I? I mean, I didn't even stick around long enough to see whether or not you wrote it all up in your ledger; I jus' took my receipt an' left it at that. Still, how was I to know you'd decide to keep the money, destroy your own counterfoil so's there'd be no record of the transaction here at the bank, an' then waltz on over to the office while I was elsewhere an' steal back my half of the receipt?'

He shook his head a little. It wouldn't have been hard: he rarely bothered to lock the office door, there was simply no need. And he'd always been careless

where paperwork was concerned. Ed had likely spotted the receipt the minute he'd let himself into the
office, sitting right where Ben had left it on his desk.
Ben himself, always too busy scratching around for
other chores to keep him occupied, had never even
realized it was gone.

'That,' said Graham, speaking hoarsely through
clenched teeth, 'is an outrageous suggestion!'

'Well, that's what larceny is,' Ben agreed tightly.
'It's an outrage, Ed. Not that I blame you. Fifteen
hundred dollars . . . that must've been quite a temptation, 'specially with the rightful owner livin' five
hundred miles away. Who'd ever get to know about
it? And who'd ever think a down-at-heel, know-
nothin' farmer'd have the gumption to come all this
way to claim it in person?' Suddenly his expression
hardened. 'Now, you gonna 'fess up, or do I ask Fred
here to check through your counterfoils? It only
takes one number to be missin' 'round about four
months ago to prove it one way or the other, Ed.'

'How *dare* you make such an accusation!' blustered Graham. 'Please, Mr Harvey—'

'Give it up,' said Ben. 'See, Fred's right: I don't
recall him handlin' the transaction, but now that I
think on it, I do remember dealin' with you, clear
enough. So I guess that's what it comes down to, Ed
– you, or me. An' I sure as hell know it wasn't *me*.'

Graham was staring at him through bug eyes
now, breathing hard, fast and shallow. He whispered, 'This . . . you can't. . . .'

And then he broke.

He let go a peculiar mixture of shriek and scream and then suddenly exploded into action, dashing forward and making a clumsy attempt to shoulder-ram Ben aside so that he could get to the door at the far end of the cage.

All at once the place was in uproar, with Graham, Jameson and Fred Harvey all yelling at once. Only Ben saved his breath, preferring action to words. He'd anticipated this, or something very much like it, and went back with the blow, at the same time shoving out one leg to trip the clerk as he blundered past.

Graham lost his footing, stumbled forward and smashed against the grille with a cold, shuddery clang – but it was going to take more than that to stop him now, and Ben knew it.

Regaining his balance, Graham reached out to shove the door open, but Ben grabbed him by one shoulder and whipped him around, and Graham, knowing the game was up, made a mewling sort of sound and swung a desperate roundhouse right that Ben quickly blocked. He threw back a short jab that caught the bank clerk on the jaw and tipped his head a little sideways, but by now Graham was so fired-up that Ben didn't suppose he even felt it.

As if to prove the suspicion, Graham came back livelier than ever and threw another punch, this one faster and more vicious than its predecessor. Ben crowded him and took it on the shoulder, where it hurt like hell. Ignoring the pain, he punched Graham in the belly, once, twice, three times, so that

Graham rose up on his toe-caps like some kind of ballet dancer before sagging on legs turned to paper. As he went down, Ben clubbed him again, this time over one ear, and the clerk collapsed in a heap, his eyes rolling up into his head.

For a moment a heavy, stunned silence filled the bank. Then—

'Y-you *killed* him!' breathed Harvey.

'Killed him, hell,' wheezed Ben, shaking his right hand to get some feeling back into it. 'I knocked him cold, is all.' He squinted over one of Harvey's meaty shoulders and said, 'Gimme a hand here, Jameson. We'll lock him in yonder vault 'til I'm ready to collect him.'

Recovering his composure, Harvey drew himself up and blocked his path. 'You'll do no such thing!' he hissed. 'In case you've forgotten the law, Marshal, Edward is innocent until proven guilty, and he'll be treated accordingly. Good grief, man, you've already beaten him senseless. Do you have to strip him of his dignity, as well?'

Ben looked at Harvey as if he couldn't believe his ears. 'He's guilty as hell,' he replied. 'Christ, he jus' tried to run for it, didn't he?'

'He ran, all right,' agreed Harvey, but only because you were bullying him!'

'Bullyin'—!'

'Yes, Marshal,' said Harvey, more firmly. 'And until I hear more than mere conjecture, I have to stand by my clerk.'

'You want proof?' asked Ben, feeling his temper slipping again. 'All right. Check your counterfoils. I'll wager that fifty-dollar pension you folks're all so set on givin' me that you'll find one missin' 'round about four months ago. An' while you're about it, take a peek in Tom Sutherland's account. It's my guess that's where you'll find at least half of Jameson's money.'

Harvey frowned. 'Tom Suth—? What the dickens has he got to do with any of this? For heaven's sake, Marshal, the man's a respected employee of Western Union! He—'

'Ed wasn't in this alone,' Ben interrupted him. 'He knew Jameson'd wire me when his money never turned up. He had to make sure I never got those wires, else the game was up.' He shrugged. 'Tom Sutherland's the only man in town who could've arranged that little trick, Fred, an' I reckon he did it, too, for a half-share o' that fifteen hundred bucks.' He eyed his companion briefly and said, 'I guess they underestimated you, Jameson, figured you'd jus' write it off when you didn't get no response from them wires you sent.'

Jameson was still staring down at Graham. 'I would've, too,' he murmured, 'had I been the down-at-heel, know-nothing farmer they took me for.'

'That was just a turn o' phrase,' Ben said hurriedly, before the other man could take offence. 'Wasn't meant personal.'

'No matter,' said Jameson. 'You were right. That is what they thought of me.' He cleared his throat and offered his hand. 'It, ah, looks as if I owe you an apology, doesn't it, Marshal?'

'Ferget it,' said Ben, shaking with him. He drew down one final, deep breath, then bent and started working his hands into Graham's armpits. 'Jus' help me here, will you? We'll get this sonofabitch locked away nice'n tight while Fred here does a little checkin' up for me, an' then we'll go see about Sutherland.'

He allowed himself a brief, grim chuckle, and hearing it, Fred Harvey paused with a ledger in his fat fists and asked shakily, 'Wh-what is it, Marshal?'

'Jus' thinkin',' replied Ben softly. 'Graham an' Sutherland. I always did think them two was thick as thieves. Guess I didn't know just how right I was, did I?'

It was quite a sight: the marshal of Kane's Crossing prodding two of the town's most respected citizens over to the jailhouse like the common criminals they were.

Startled townsfolk, just beginning to venture back out on to the muggy plankwalks, stopped and stared at the spectacle. A few called out to ask what was going on. But Ben, looking neither left nor right, just kept his prisoners shuffling wretchedly ahead of him.

Beside him, Arthur Jameson shook his head in silent wonder. He hadn't really known *what* to expect when he finally reached Kane's Crossing. *Trouble*, certainly, for he had come all this way to make a serious and quite possibly dangerous accusation. But nothing could have prepared him for the events of this turbulent lunchtime.

While he and the marshal locked the unconscious Ed Graham inside the walk-in vault, the bank manager, Fred Harvey, began to work his way back through his clerk's old receipt books, and soon came up one counterfoil short. Just as the marshal had predicted, the dates on the counterfoils to either side of the missing slip confirmed that it related to business conducted some four months earlier. A subsequent check of the bank's records showed that a sum of $750 had been credited to the account of this man Sutherland just days later.

None of them felt inclined to dismiss these facts as mere coincidence.

The balance of Jameson's money had yet to come to light, but Fred Harvey, himself now convinced of Graham's guilt, suspected that the clerk had secretly opened an account for himself under a false name. He seemed confident that he would be able to find it without too much trouble, but before he embarked upon his search, he took Jameson aside to assure him that the bank was as much a victim in this business as he was himself. He had obviously started to consider the broader picture at last, and was anxious to avoid bad publicity.

'I have no wish to make things any more difficult than they need to be,' Jameson replied, much to Harvey's relief. 'I'm happy just to take my money – plus whatever interest has accrued over the last four months, of course.'

'Of course, sir,' simpered Harvey, 'of course.'

Having satisfied himself with the strength of the

circumstantial evidence Harvey had unearthed, Marshal Crawford finally set out for the Western Union office further along the street. 'You don't have to be in on this, you know,' he'd said as the bank manager fell behind them. 'I'll see that justice is served, don't you fret.'

'I've come this far,' Jameson replied. He glanced curiously at Crawford's profile and said carefully, 'May I take it he's not exactly a friend of yours, then, this man Sutherland?'

'What makes you say that?'

'Because it strikes me that you're actually looking forward to arresting him.'

'Upholdin' the law, is all,' the marshal intoned gravely.

But Jameson was right. Ben *was* looking forward to arresting Tom Sutherland. That grudge-toting sonofabitch had been a burr 'neath his saddle ever since they'd locked horns the night of the lynch-mob. Sutherland had never forgiven Ben for making him back down in front of all those potential voters, and had fared disastrously in the mayoral elections a few months later. Ben had always felt that Sutherland held him personally responsible for that.

Certainly the Western Union man had used his position on the town council to make life as awkward as possible for him ever since. He'd blocked Ben's every request – for a raise in his salary, for better street-lighting, for the appointment of a temporary deputy so he could take Nora to see some fancy doctors in Santa Fe. . . . And he had a strong suspicion that it had been Sutherland, still smarting even six years on, who'd first put up the notion that they kick him out of office to save money.

That being the case, then yeah, he *was* looking forward to arresting Sutherland. But he should've known better than to let it show.

That, however, was easier said than done.

He let himself into the poky little Western Union office and went up to the chest-high, plank-wide counter that cut the dingy little place in half. Behind the counter, Tom Sutherland was just finishing his lunch, a thick beef sandwich. He was seated at a combination workbench and desk, digging at the spaces between his teeth with a thin, sharp pick. A stack of yellow message slips sat to one side of him, his well-worn telegrapher's key directly in front.

Sutherland, Jameson saw, was a stocky man in smart grey pants, a matching vest and green sleeve-protectors. He still had a white kerchief tucked into his celluloid collar to keep his shirt clean. He was somewhere in his middle-thirties, with a wide, pale face, a light scattering of freckles and a fair, neatly trimmed beard.

Glancing up at the newcomers, he offered, without noticeable warmth, ' 'Afternoon, Marshal. May I help you?'

Ben nodded. 'Like for you to send a wire up the line to your boss, Tom,' he replied easily. As a puzzled frown creased Sutherland's brow, he squinted into thin air and dictated haltingly, ' "Have been arrested on charges of attempted larceny. Please send replacement".' Then he frowned. 'No, hold that, Tom,' he said, and his expression was so serious that Jameson couldn't suppress a smile. ' "Please send *honest* replacement",' he amended after a moment's thought. 'That's better.'

Sutherland came slowly to his feet, his dark eyes glittering dangerously as he tugged the kerchief-cum-napkin free. 'Is this some idea of a joke?' he asked.

'No,' said Ben, 'it's not.' And then, his voice becoming a deep, authoritative snap: 'Tom Sutherland, I'm arrestin' you for conspirin' to cheat this here feller out of money that rightfully belongs to him, an' I got me a strong feelin' that Western Union might jus' decide to add a few more charges when they find out about all them wires you made sure I never got to see.'

Alarm showed momentarily in Sutherland's eyes, and his jaw muscles worked briefly, but when he spoke his voice was cool and disparaging. 'Have you finally lost your senses, Crawford?'

'Never felt better,' countered Ben. 'Now, you send that wire, you hear me? An' make a good job of it, Tom, 'cause it's gonna be the last damn' wire you send for a real long time.'

The telegram sent, Sutherland shrugged stiffly into his suit jacket and let himself through the flap in the counter. 'I don't know what it is you're accusing me of,' he lied, 'but I'll fight it every step of the way, Marshal. I'm not without influence, you know. Whatever case you think you've got against me, my lawyer will tear it to shreds.'

'He's welcome to try,' replied Ben. 'But we've got the evidence, Tom. An' if Ed Graham decides to make a full confession – you know, so's the judge'll go a mite easier on him when it comes to sentencin' – then your lawyer'll need to be a damn' *miracle* worker to get you off.'

Sutherland went pale. Clearly he hadn't considered the possibility that his co-conspirator might testify against him in order to save his own skin. All at once he got that hunted animal look, and his fists started clenching.

'Steady, now,' Ben warned him. 'You know what happened the last time you took a swing at me.'

Together, he and Jameson walked their prisoner along to the bank, opened the vault and collected the groggy but recovering Graham. Then Ben herded them both along, side by side, over to the jailhouse.

They were about halfway across the street when a new voice called Ben's name. This, he knew, was one voice he couldn't ignore, so he broke stride and called for his prisoners to hold up a minute, and turned around just as Conrad Kane came hustling through the dust, his expression one of confusion as he looked at Sutherland and Graham.

'Ben!' he gasped, not used to moving so fast. 'What the devil—?'

Ben cut him off with one raised palm. 'I can

explain,' he replied. 'But let's get in off the street first.'

Jameson, now feeling somewhat redundant, said quickly, 'Well, if you'll excuse me, Marshal. It's been quite a day, and I think I'd better get myself a room for the night.'

Ben nodded. 'Sure. Stop by for your case any time, Jameson.'

'Jameson?' repeated Kane, frowningly.

Ben made the introductions. As they shook hands, Jameson said, 'You have a heck of a lawman here, Mr Kane. A man who really gets the job done.'

'Yes,' agreed Kane, still baffled. 'Ben—'

'One thing at a time,' said Ben, secretly warming to the praise. 'Let's get these here miscreants behind bars first.'

'You've got to help us, Conrad,' called Sutherland, a little desperately. 'The man's lost his senses—'

'One more comment like that,' said Ben, 'an' you'll be losin' your *teeth*.'

'Ben . . .' Kane muttered warningly.

Ben got his prisoners moving again, and, as he followed along in their wake, he walked somehow taller and prouder than he had in many a year: just like a real, live lawman, in fact. When he moved ahead to shove open the office door, however, he came back to earth with a bump.

Someone had called by in his absence . . . and torn the place apart.

SIX

'Just what the devil's going on here, Ben?'

It was five minutes later, and once he'd gotten over the shock of finding the jailhouse turned upside-down, Ben had locked his prisoners in the communal cell and rejoined Kane in the ruined office outside.

Now he surveyed the damage more closely and, lips clamping tight, shook his head in disbelief. His unwelcome visitor must have worked himself into a frenzy to have caused so much destruction. The cluttered desk had been swept clean, and discarded paperwork now littered every inch of the plank floor. The old writing bureau had been kicked in, the filing cabinet toppled sideways and over. The two visitor's chairs had been smashed to matchwood against the walls, and the funnel leading from the stove up through the low ceiling had been wrenched free at its lowest join to spray soot and dust everywhere. Finally, the coffee pot had been hurled violently against the right-hand wall. Now it sat behind the door, dented and mis-shapen, and the room itself stank of the beverage it had so recently contained.

'Ben?' prodded Kane.

Ben drew air in through his nostrils and half-whispered, 'Jared Parsons.'

Kane's dark hazel eyes saucered. '*What*?'

'He's out,' Ben explained grimly. 'An' I figure he's been sneakin' around town since sun-up.'

Briefly he told the mayor about the dead chicken and the pot-shot his unseen tormentor had taken at him. When he was finished, Kane had to grope for a response, for shock had slowed his usually agile mind. 'I don't, I mean . . . *why*, Ben? Why come back here? Why *do* all these things?'

'Why'd the sonofabitch do *any* of what he did?' countered Ben.

Still, it was a valid question. Why *had* Jared Parsons come back to torment him, today of all days? All he'd ever done was save the sick-minded bastard from a lynch-mob. But maybe he, Ben, had been sniffing around the wrong tree all this time, and blaming Jared for the actions of some other party.

All this while, Kane had been thinking, too. 'Well,' he said, a little shakily, 'we've got to find him, Ben, and fast! It's a big day for the town. For you. We can't let Jared spoil it.' He paced a small circle, a neat, cherubic-looking man in a well-cut pale-grey suit. 'I'll get some of the men together,' he decided, talking more to himself than to Ben. 'We'll comb the town from top to bottom till we find him.'

'You won't flush him out that way,' predicted Ben, his voice like steel. 'For one thing, he'd spot *us* a long time before we spotted him. For another, you're askin' for trouble, you arm a bunch of townsmen and send 'em off on a manhunt; they're more likely to wind up shootin' each other, if not themselves.'

'Then what do we do?' implored Kane. 'We've got to do something!'

'You leave Jared to me,' said Ben. 'I'll find him. An' if I don't . . . well, I reckon he'll find *me*, sooner or later. In any case, Jared's not the only problem we got right now.'

Kane threw a glance at the cell-block door, suddenly remembering what had brought about this meeting in the first place. 'That's a point,' he said. 'What's the idea, arresting Graham and Sutherland?'

'Ferget Graham an' Sutherland. They're small-fry. We got us another little complication, Conrad.'

Fearing the worst, Kane said, 'What now?'

Wearily Ben told Kane all about Alex McGivern and the three men who were hunting him. Kane seemed to shrink beneath the weight of this new problem. 'Do you think they'll ride on?' he asked hopefully, when Ben fell silent again. 'When they don't find this man McGivern here, I mean?'

Ben shrugged. 'It's possible. But it'd be better for McGivern if it was to end right here.'

Kane frowned. 'You mean arrest them?'

'I mean *brace* 'em,' replied Ben, knowing there were no charges he could bring against the Elliotts and Patch Samuels without hard evidence.

Kane paled, shook his head again and held up both hands, palms out. 'No way! I won't allow it, Ben! One man against three, and all for the sake of a stranger?'

'Well,' Ben reminded him, 'that's what lawmen do, Conrad. We stand up for the folks who can't stand up for themselves.' A cool smile suddenly touched his mouth, and he added, 'Hell, that's why you hired me in the first place, isn't it?'

Ignoring the barb, Kane said, 'For God's sake, man, no one expects you to risk your life on your last day in office!'

'You people pay me to uphold the law,' Ben said doggedly. 'That's what I aim to do.'

'The only thing you're aiming to do,' spat Kane, 'is get yourself *killed*!'

'Gettin' killed's not part o' the plan,' Ben replied gruffly. ' 'Sides, I ain't decided for sure which way I'm fixin' to play this yet.' In truth, he was still torn by his desire to grab this one last chance at glory, and his responsibility toward Nora. He owed her so much, everything, in fact, and couldn't bear the thought of her having to live the rest of her life as a widow if, as Kane had just said, he went and got himself killed.

'Well,' said Kane, calming down a bit. 'We've got to do something, Ben. What do you suggest?'

'We'll let McGivern's problem simmer for a while. He should be safe enough at my place, 'long as Frank an' Mike keep their mouths shut. Meantime,

I'll take a stroll around town, see if I can't get a lead on Jared.'

'Watch yourself, then,' said Kane, his concern touchingly genuine. 'We don't want to lose you now, of all times, do we?'

Ben dredged up a warmer smile for his companion. 'Now, you keep all this under your hat, Conrad,' he warned. 'Less people who know about Jared, the better.'

'All right,' said the mayor, grudgingly. And ironically, he added, 'You're the one with the shield.'

They left the wrecked office together, and as Kane hurried back to his loan agency, Ben made a point of locking the thick oak and strap-steel door behind him. He didn't think that Jared would touch the jailhouse again, there was no point, but with an unpredictable cuss like that, you never knew for sure. Besides, he figured his prisoners were entitled to some protection, at least.

As he pocketed the key, he glanced thoughtfully back toward Macy's, and knew a moment of increased tension when he realized the Elliott and Samuels horses were no longer tied up outside the saloon. The time for refreshment, it seemed, was over. Now those boys were going on the hunt.

Without warning his stomach growled, reminding him that he hadn't eaten since breakfast. But he still didn't have much of an appetite. The McGivern business, in particular, had put him in a quandary. He genuinely wanted to help the former Pinkerton man, but all he kept seeing in his mind was Nora,

Nora saying, 'You won't do anything silly, will you?'

Well, he certainly didn't plan on doing anything like that. But he had to do *something*. It wasn't in his nature to simply turn a blind eye and trust that McGivern would take his troubles away with him the minute he was strong enough to ride. And yet Ben knew that no one would blame him if he did decide to sit this one out. Kane had pretty much said it all just now. *One man against three, and all for the sake of a stranger? For God's sake, man, no one expects you to risk your life on your last day in office.*

No, he thought, nobody expected it, not even McGivern. But Ben expected it of himself, expected no less . . . and there was the problem. It all came down to a question of loyalty: of whether he would, in the end, be true to himself, or true to Nora.

Readjusting the set of the embossed, double-loop holster on his hip, he headed along to O'Driscoll's place, his eyes moving restlessly all the while, constantly searching for any sign of Jared. When he finally reached his destination, he saw Mike sitting on a barrel down at the far end of the stable, picking at a modest lunch of bread and cheese that was spread out on a gingham napkin on his lap.

Glancing around and recognizing his visitor, O'Driscoll quickly gathered the food up into a bundle, sprang to his feet and demanded, 'What's going on, Ben? Frank Landis came hustling in here—'

'You get rid of the horse?' Ben cut in, giving the place a quick once-over to confirm as much for himself.

O'Driscoll nodded. 'Tethered him down along Masterson Creek,' he replied. 'He'll be safe enough there, I reckon. But what's—?'

'Anyone come by, askin' after him?'

Sidetracked again, O'Driscoll said, 'Three men. Nice fellers, by the looks.'

'What did you tell 'em?'

'What Frank *told* me to tell them. That I didn't know what they were talking about.'

'An' they believed you?'

'Well . . . I *guess*.'

'Good.' Ben thought briefly, then asked, 'How long ago were they here?'

'Ten, fifteen minutes.'

'Did they leave their horses?'

'No. I think they turned them out in the public corral.'

Ben digested that. It meant they weren't sure just how long they figured on sticking around, yet. 'Did you see where they went when they left here?'

'Not really. Turned left, I think.'

That made sense. Left would take them up to Frank's hotel, surely their next port of call. Keeping his expression neutral, Ben said, 'How'd they strike you, them boys? Like they was liquored-up?'

He desperately wanted the answer to be yes, because if they'd allowed one too many beers to dull their senses, that would make his decision about how best to deal with them all the easier to reach. But O'Driscoll said, 'Nope.' Then, impatiently: 'What *is* going on, Ben?'

His mind elsewhere, Ben said, 'Tell you later.'

He turned and walked back out into the full, enervating heat of early afternoon. On the other side of the street, laughing, chattering women were organizing the picnic, throwing checkered cloths over trestle tables and setting out little bowls in which they'd arranged wild flowers. Drawing a shuddery breath at the sight, he shook his head and retraced his steps up to Frank's hotel.

He was about thirty yards from the place when he saw Arthur Jameson come out on to the plankwalk, pause briefly, and then start heading for the jailhouse. Increasing the pace as much as his arthritis would allow, Ben closed the distance between them and, when he was near enough, called out the Nebraskan's name. Jameson broke stride, looked over one shoulder and quickly trotted back to him. 'Marshal,' he breathed. 'The very man.'

'You'll be wantin' your case, I guess?' said Ben. 'An' that pesky little derringer o' yourn?'

Jameson gave an awkward, indecisive shrug. 'Well, I'm not really sure.' Hooking a thumb back the way he'd just come, he said, 'I've been over at the hotel all this while, waiting to check in, but there doesn't seem to be anyone around to give me a room.'

'What?'

'The place seems . . . *deserted*,' Jameson muttered.

The word echoed in Ben's mind. It sounded so sinister that something hard and cold suddenly filled his empty belly, and he turned and hurried back toward the hotel. He went inside, up to the desk and palmed the shiny brass bell urgently to get some attention. When that didn't work, he went around the counter and into the poky little room behind it, where Frank stored clean linen and did all his book-keeping. The room was empty, the back door, through which he and Doc Warren had carried McGivern earlier in the day, ominously ajar.

He quickly scanned the room, then crossed it and glanced out into the alleyway beyond. This too was empty.

He went back inside, across the lobby and over to the staircase, where he peered up and called Frank's name.

There was no reply.

A noise made him turn toward the entrance just as Jameson came back inside. Reading something in Ben's behaviour, the farmer said hesitantly, 'Is everything all right, Marshal?'

Ben didn't waste time replying. His mind was already racing ahead, considering what had most likely happened here, and what was *still* to happen elsewhere. He pushed past Jameson, forcing his stiff joints to move and to hell with the pain, and started crossing the street at a lumbering run, pulling up once when a startled horsebacker suddenly crossed his path.

Seconds later, First Street fell behind him and a patchwork of alleyways and dog-trots opened up ahead. No longer used to such exertion, he started flagging almost at once, and his belly, once flat and taut, now rose and fell, rose and fell, to wear him down still faster. Again he hated himself for having grown old and unfit, for no longer being the man he used to be, but it was too late for that now: the damage had already been done.

He took a right, went across an intersection with yellow dust exploding around his pounding boots, and he told himself that he was doing pretty well. But the awful truth was that he was slowing down with every step he took, and finding it increasingly difficult to breathe.

At last he fell against the corner of a dumpy adobe house, grabbed at the whitewashed stone and moaned with the effort of drawing air down into lungs that felt hot and raw. Little red lights speared his eyeballs. Sweat beaded his face and darkened the armpits of his bib shirt. But a moment later he forced himself to push on, his run little more than a glorified stumble now.

He wheeled right, into a narrow, deserted side-street flanked by more adobe houses, then left, into another, and then, all at once, he saw them not more than thirty or forty yards ahead of him, four figures moving line abreast down towards the little flat-roofed, single-storey house on the outskirts of town that he shared with Nora. Three of them were pushing forward in a confident swagger, clearly eager to reach their destination and get on with the blood-letting. The fourth was stumbling and weaving, much like Ben himself.

He slowed down, still wheezing like a rain-filled

accordion, and flipped the restraining thong off the
hammer of the Whitney without once taking his
eyes off the men he was just about to brace. And he
was going to brace them now: they'd left him no
choice.

Johnny Elliott was down at the far end of the line,
looking tall and lean in his corduroy jacket and
Kentucky jeans. Beside him came brother Matthew,
shorter, slighter, with longer blond hair and spur-
hung Justin boots that made music Ben could hear
even at this distance.

The chunky man who was doing all the stagger-
ing was Frank Landis, and Ben hated to think what
they'd done to make him betray McGivern's where-
abouts. Patch Samuels, the next man in line, had
one hand clamped around Frank's right arm, and
was pretty much dragging at him to keep him
moving.

Gaining on them now, Ben watched as they began
to cross the wide, scrub-littered expanse of open
ground that separated his house from all the others.
It was easy enough to guess at what had happened:
that when it came to it, Frank had shown himself to
be a lousy liar, and that the Elliotts and Patch
Samuels had quickly seen or sensed as much and
forced the truth out of him, most likely at gunpoint.
Then, having discovered the location of the man
they'd come all this way to kill, they'd dragged him
out into the alleyway behind the hotel and made
him show them the way to Ben's house.

Yeah, he told himself grimly, it was all clear

enough. But right now his thoughts were dominated by another consideration: Nora. Nora, who stood to witness a cold-blooded execution at best, and maybe get caught in the cross-fire at worst.

Squaring his shoulders, increasing the pace again, he tore the Whitney from leather and yelled, '*That's far enough, boys!*'

Almost as one, the men ahead of him drew up and heeled around, and as Ben got his first good look at Frank's blood-smudged face, he felt a hot spear of anger course through him.

Frank looked like hell. His crinkly grey hair was mussed and dishevelled. There were ugly purple swellings around his left eye and both lips, and lines of crusted blood – they looked black at this distance – scoring the sweated flesh around his nostrils and mouth. There was more blood on his shirt and the charcoal-grey vest he wore over it, little splashes no bigger than half-dimes.

Seeing that, seeing *all* of it, Ben's teeth set hard and his breathing quickened as the anger in him continued to feed on itself, for this was his town these owlhoots had invaded, this beaten man was a citizen he had sworn to protect, and inside the house behind them – his house – was his wife, and a man who had just undergone surgery and was in no fit state to defend himself.

Now, with the distance between them halved, Ben finally hauled to a stop and planted himself with legs spread wide for balance, and Frank, seeing him, seemed to sag in on himself with relief. No longer caught up in Patch Samuels' grasp, he took a shambling step forward and said thickly, 'I'm sorry, Marshal. I couldn't . . . I *had* to tell them—'

' 'S'all right, Frank,' Ben called back. 'You jus' move off a pace, now. I'll take care o' things here.'

Johnny Elliott's grey, almond-shaped eyes moved up from the Whitney in Ben's hand to the bleak promise of violence in his face, and he said warningly, 'You'll stay outa this, Marshal, that's what you'll do. We don't want no trouble, an' I don't reckon you do either, not with you bein' so close to retirement an' all. All we want is the Pinkerton man. Then we'll be gone, an' you'll never see us again.'

'I got a better idea,' said Ben, watching them all closely as Frank hobbled out of the firing line, hugging his ribs carefully. 'You boys give it up. You broke the law an' you got away with it, all but your pa, who was caught fair an' square an' paid the price. You jus' learn your lesson from that an' call it a day.'

'We'll call it a day,' said Patch Samuels, 'soon as we've done for McGivern.'

Ben let his pent-up breath go in a shallow sigh. 'I won't give you boys a second chance,' he cautioned.

'Marshal,' Johnny spat back. 'We don't even plan on givin' you *one* chance.'

And, acting in unison, he and his kin went for their guns.

Not for one moment had Ben expected anything else. He'd known all along that this confrontation would come to shooting sooner or later, that some of

them would die here this day, and all in the name of
a misguided vengeance. Johnny and the others had
simply come too far, and craved their idea of justice
too badly, for it to end any other way.

And so, he responded in kind.

As Patch Samuels dropped to a crouch and went
for the Smith & Wesson Russian on his hip, Ben shot
him twice in the chest, and the one-eyed man went
backwards with blood erupting from his wounds in
a fine red spray. Samuels' sugarloaf sombrero went
flying as the man himself slammed hard against the
dirt, and he squirmed briefly until, quite suddenly,
his legs stiffened. Then he stopped moving altogether.

By that time, the air was quivering with gunfire.
Young Matthew had cleared leather faster than Ben
had expected and was standing his ground, his left
hand a blur of motion as he fanned the Merwin &
Hulbert Army .44 in his other fist.

Shrinking in on himself, thinking only of survival
now, Ben dodged to the left, fetched up against the
nearest wall, dropped to a crouch and sent a single
shot back at him. More by accident than design, the
.36-calibre bullet burned into the fleshy upper part
of Matthew's right leg, and the kid screamed as it
buckled under him and sent him sideways and
down.

His mind racing now, Ben quickly took stock. One
dead, one down and Johnny's Peacemaker still blaz-
ing away at him.

He figured it could've been worse.

A flurry of slugs tore at the wall barely more than a foot above his head, powdering his hat and shoulders with dust. Twisting, he came up and quickly drew a bead on his still-active opponent. In the instant before he squeezed the trigger again, he saw that the mouth beneath Johnny's blond steerhorn moustache was yanked wide in a scream of defiance.

He loosed off his fourth shot.

It missed, but came close enough to remind Johnny just how vulnerable he was right there in the middle of all that open ground. All at once the tall man in the high-crowned brown hat turned and started running for the only cover available, Ben's house, moving with the awkward, pigeon-toed sprint of a man whose horse usually does all the work for him, and Ben himself swore hard.

He struggled erect and went after the fleeing man, his thoughts focusing on Nora again, and he knew that they were finished, all of them, if Johnny reached the house, for he could hole up nicely in there. McGivern would be at his mercy, and Nora would make a handsome hostage with which to negotiate his freedom once the Pinkerton man was dead.

A movement off to one side suddenly penetrated his feverish thinking, and he heard a hoarse voice, Frank's, bawling his name. In the next moment Johnny's kid brother sat up from where he'd been writhing with the pain of his wounded leg, took aim and started fanning his .44 again.

Ben just had time to curse him before something

hard and hot punched him in the right arm, midway between shoulder and elbow, and he staggered a little and spun to face the freckle-faced youngster as a streak of ragged white fire tore through him.

'*Marshal*!' Frank yelled again.

Matthew was struggling to get up, his face still twisted in agony, his bloody right leg held straight and stiff beneath him, and he was halfway there when he realized that he hadn't hit Ben as fatally as he'd thought: that Ben was still standing tall. For a merest part of a second their eyes met, Ben's pale blue and glazing fast, Matthew's an almond-shaped grey. Then Matthew brought his .44 up again and Ben shot him in the face.

Matthew's head exploded in a red cloud, he back-pedalled maybe six, eight feet, discharged his gun one final time into the ground, then collapsed.

There was a moment then when everything except the pain in Ben's arm seemed to just . . . stop, and Johnny, hearing the sudden, violent exchange of shots behind him, hauled in and turned around to witness the outcome of the contest for himself.

He didn't like what he saw.

All at once, his desire to reach the house was eclipsed by a stronger desire to kill the man who'd just killed his brother. He started screaming again and jabbed his .45 back at Ben, and knowing that the Whitney was empty now, Ben flung the pistol aside and threw himself to the ground fast.

He landed hard beside the corpse of Patch Samuels, and the impact of it woke a fresh wave of pain in his wounded arm that made him want to puke. But puking was a luxury he couldn't afford right then. Instead, he grabbed left-handed for the dead man's Smith & Wesson, brought it up and started returning fire.

With .44-calibre bullets spanging and whining all around him, Johnny suddenly broke to the right and started running again, this time hoping to lose himself in the maze of side-streets that bordered a brush-filled vacant lot to the west. Ben shoved up again, his right shirt-sleeve soaked black with blood, and started after him, yelling to Frank, 'Get inside! Make sure Nora's all right!'

He felt really dreadful now, with blood pounding in his ears and his throat closed so tight that he could barely draw breath, but he forced himself to keep going, because if Johnny got clear now, this thing would never be over for McGivern, or any of them.

Up ahead, blundering through tall dry grass like a man trying to wade across a fast-flowing stream, Johnny quickly reloaded his Peacemaker on the run, thinking fast and knowing he must turn the tables on his pursuer or die in the attempt. He threw a glance back over one shoulder, received a distorted image of Ben about twenty-some yards away, stumble-running after him, and suddenly, his mind made up, he stopped, turned, thrust the Peacemaker out and shot his pursuer in the head.

The sound of the gunblast rocked across the vacant lot, and Ben cried out, twitched, lost his hat and corkscrewed to earth. As he went down, Johnny Elliott knew a moment of sheer, animal joy at his victory, but in the very next moment he remembered his brother and cousin, and their pa, and his handsome face tightened with the knowledge that, suddenly, he was all alone in the world.

Shoving that thought aside, he started back the way he'd just come, shoulders slumped and breathing hard. With Crawford dead, there was no one else to stop him from returning to the marshal's house and finishing the job that had brought them here in the first place. Then, with McGivern finally on his way to Hell, he could start thinking about taking Matthew and Patch back home for a decent burial—

Suddenly he pulled up sharp, the tall grass whispering and rustling around his long legs.

No more than ten yards ahead of him now, the marshal had started pushing up out of the waist-high weeds, his movements slow and uncertain, his bloodshot eyes clearly unfocused. He was bleeding from a crease above his left eye, and his face was the colour of old parchment.

Johnny brought the Peacemaker up again, but held his fire. One glance told him that the marshal posed no immediate threat. From the looks of it, his hasty bullet had just knocked the old lawdog down and scrambled his thinking for a while. Indeed, the sledge-hammer blow had left him so disorientated that he wasn't even aware that Johnny was still there, watching him.

Johnny shook his head, his upper lip curling

disdainfully as he started wading forward again. He came to a halt beside the lawman and said softly, 'You're a hard man to kill, I'll grant you that, you sonofabitch.'

Then he lifted the Peacemaker again, so that the short barrel was no more than six inches away from Ben's left ear.

He said, 'So long.'

And again, gun-thunder rolled across the lot.

But it was Johnny Elliott who felt the spinning smack of hot lead. It came out of nowhere to rip him off his feet and throw him backwards, the slug making a deceptively small entry hole just about where his right nipple must be, and an altogether bigger and bloodier exit wound to one side of his spine.

The gunblast helped to sharpen Ben's addled thinking a bit, but he was still curiously detached from the events going on around him. As he reached up to sleeve blood off his forehead, however, he heard a rustle of dry grass someplace behind him, and the sound of peculiar, uneven footsteps coming slowly closer. A few moments later, a grey shadow fell across one of his shoulders, the shadow of a man carrying a rifle.

Still struggling to bring order back to his jumbled thoughts, he turned his head and squinted up at his saviour, but the bullet-crease had temporarily distorted and doubled his vision, and all he got was a blurred impression of a man that was further softened and fogged by the sunlight that kept winking and flashing over one of his shoulders.

'He . . . he dead?' husked Ben.

'Don't come much deader,' said the other man.

Ben's eyelids fluttered. It was over, then. 'Help me up, here . . .' he said.

'Nope,' replied the other man. 'I help you up, you're like to fall right down again. Best you stay where you are for a while.'

Ben shook his head – which was a bad mistake – and then swallowed. 'Hell with that,' he persisted. 'Gimme a hand here. Reckon I owe you one, Mr. . . ?'

'I don't want your thanks, Marshal,' said the other man, and he made a soft, snickering kind of sound that suddenly put Ben on his guard. 'I got my own reasons for keepin' you alive.'

Ben frowned, and as the shadow on the ground in front of him turned and slid away, and he heard the peculiar, uneven sound of its footsteps again, he realized with a sickening kind of lurch just who it was he'd been talking to.

'*Jared!*' he yelled through clenched teeth, and started patting at the grass to locate his fallen .44. '*Come back here you sonofabitch! Come back here, Jared Parsons!*'

SEVEN

'I swear, Ben,' muttered Doc Warren, as he put the finishing touches to the bandage around his patient's tender forehead, 'what with one thing and another, you've given me my busiest day since I can't remember when.' His thin, sallow face worked in a rare smile. 'Thanks – I *think.*'

Ben managed laconically, 'Jus' don't expect me to make a habit of it, that's all.'

While Doc went off to help Nora tend to Frank Landis, he tried to settle himself more comfortably on the horsehair sofa and closed his eyes. Around him, the parlour was now so quiet that he could easily hear the frantic ticking of the cheap little shelf clock in the kitchen, even above all the pernickety little *oohs* and *ahhs* that Frank made as Doc examined him.

By contrast, the previous hour had been a riot of activity which had left him in a daze, but at least the buzzing in his sore head was finally starting to fade, and he found himself more able to take stock at last.

By the time his vision had cleared sufficiently for him to get his good hand around the grips of Patch Samueis' Smith & Wesson, Jared Parsons was long gone. That didn't stop Ben from making several attempts to rise and go after him, of course – but even when he finally managed to get his feet under him, it was all he could do just to keep his balance, and as much as it hurt to do so, he had to concede defeat.

Luckily, a handful of the more courageous towns-folk had put in an appearance by then, and helping hands were soon reaching out to hold him steady, while a whole flurry of curious, concerned voices started bombarding him from all sides.

'You all right, Marshal? You're bleeding!'

'Ay, and that's a heckuva gash you've got above your eye.'

'What's been going on, Marshal?'

'Yeah. What was all that shooting, Ben?'

And then: 'Judas Priest! There's a *dead* man over here!'

The new arrivals waded through the tall grass to get a closer look at the late Johnny Elliott, upon whose bloody chest fat blow-flies were already feasting, and a shuddery sigh whispered through Ben's dry lips as he forced himself to let go of all the tension that had built up during the fight, and was still making the muscles in his arms and legs knot up. He thought about the killing he'd done and whether or not it could have been avoided, and then he looked down at his blood-soaked right arm and wondered how bad the damage really was.

Pretty soon after that the townsfolk started leading him back home. He felt weak as a kitten now, and would have spewed, had he had anything in his belly to bring up.

A sudden hush fell over the little crowd when they reached his house and spotted the bodies of Matthew Elliott and Patch Samuels, still sprawled where they had fallen. Once again Ben was struck by the absolute waste of it all, and could only shake his head at the dead men.

There was a stir then, as Conrad Kane came running. He too broke stride when he spotted the bodies, then hurried on through the little gathering until he reached Ben. 'Ben!' he cried anxiously. 'For God's sake, man! Are you all right?'

Ben looked at him and nodded. 'Uh-huh.'

Heedless of all the blood, Kane got one arm around him and helped him on toward the house. 'Don't you fret about any of this,' he said, meaning the bodies. 'I'll deal with everything.' And then, a little louder: 'Has anyone here sent for Doc Warren yet?'

'Hank Teale just went for him,' someone replied.

The door to the house opened as they came closer, and Nora wheeled herself out to meet them. Ben saw that her heart-shaped face was even paler than usual, her lips were quivering and she was having a heckuva time trying to hold back the tears that were even now making her well-spaced hazel eyes shine.

'Ben . . .' she finally managed in a strangled little

voice. 'Oh Ben, look at the *state* of you. . . .'

'I'm all right,' he said, and sagged a bit in Kane's grip.

What followed after that was a fragmented blur. For a time there was nothing but confusion. Ben slumped down onto the sofa beside the cold fireplace and fell into a light doze with Nora holding his good hand as if she might never let it go. Then Doc arrived and Kane started to give orders for the removal of the bodies, and gradually the house emptied out. Opening his eyes again, Ben hooked a thumb wearily towards the kitchen, where Frank was sitting at the table, holding his head in his hands. He said, 'I can wait. See to Frank first.'

But Doc ignored that. 'You've been shot,' he replied. 'Frank hasn't.'

'*I'll* make a start on Frank,' said Nora. Having satisfied herself that Ben was in no immediate danger, she had calmed down a little and was starting to think practically again, like the experienced lawman's wife that she was.

As she wheeled herself from the room, Ben allowed Doc to help him out of his bloody shirt and then submitted to the medic's careful probings while he drank a bitter white solution that Doc had dissolved in a glass of water.

Eventually Doc declared, 'You're a lucky man, Ben. The bullet passed right through your arm, which means I don't have to go hunting around for it, just need to clean it and plug it. As for this crease above your eye . . . I bet it hurts like the devil, doesn't it?'

Ben tried unsuccessfully to shrug. 'You're the doctor,' he grunted. '*You* tell *me*.'

'Well, that powder I just gave you should help with that. Should settle that ache in your arm, too.'

While Doc worked on him, Ben said, 'How's . . . McGivern?'

'I'm quietly confident,' replied Doc.

'Well, that's . . . somethin', I guess.'

He fell silent again, his thoughts suddenly returning to Jared.

But for that sonofabitch, he'd be dead by now. The thought made him feel uneasy, on two counts. First, the fact that Jared had turned up at such a propitious moment implied that he'd been keeping tabs on Ben all day. Hell, he might even be watching the house right this minute! Secondly, he had bought into that fight just now for one reason and one reason only: to keep Ben alive until he was good and ready to kill him himself.

'There,' Doc announced at last, and started to help him shrug carefully into a fresh white shirt. 'That should hold you.' He held up one hand in front of Ben's face and said, 'How many fingers am I holding up, Ben?'

Ben sighed irritably while he fumbled one-handed with the buttons. 'S'all right, Doc. I'm fine now.'

'Just answer the question.'

'Two.'

'And now?'

'One.'

'All right. Now follow my finger without moving your head. . . .'

Knowing it would do no good to resist, Ben did as he was told, and Doc seemed to be pleased with the results. 'Now, you try taking things easy for a few days,' he advised. 'Get some food inside you, sleep for a few hours, and take another powder if that headache gets any worse. I'll drop by again in the morning and change those dressings.'

He disappeared into the kitchen to help Nora with Frank, and Ben closed his eyes again. Dizzy with blood-loss, he dozed fitfully for a short time, until a discreet tapping at the front door roused him again. When he opened his eyes, he saw Conrad Kane peering at him from around the parlour doorframe.

The mayor looked from the bandage at his head to the sling in which his right arm was suspended and said, 'You up to visitors, Ben?'

'Sure.'

Coming deeper into the room, Kane said confidentially, 'I've had the bodies taken down to Holden's.' Vic Holden was the town's mortician, strangely enough a man of enormous good humour. 'We'll get them into the ground before sundown.'

'Good.'

'How are you feeling?'

'I'll live long enough to collect that gold watch, don't you fret,' Ben replied with poor grace.

'I hope to heck you do,' Kane agreed fervently, and once again Ben was touched by his very genuine concern. All the years he'd known Kane, he'd tended to dismiss him as just another politician. Now, though, he was seeing him in a different light, and he liked what he saw. 'Still,' muttered the mayor, 'we'll have to postpone the picnic 'til you're better.'

Ben frowned. The picnic. He'd forgotten about that. 'After all the fussyfyin' that's been goin' on all day?' he asked. 'No way, Conrad. You folks go ahead an' enjoy yourselves. I don't have to be there.'

'Ben, you're the guest of *honour*!'

Ben was about to voice another caustic retort when suddenly he fell silent. Glancing thoughtfully at his wounded arm, he murmured, 'So I am.' And a moment later he said, 'All right. Let's get the damn' thing over an' done with, then.'

Kane made no secret of his surprise. 'You're not telling me you feel up to it, surely?'

'Why not? All I need's a couple hours' rest.'

Kane's voice dropped lower and he flicked a meaningful glance toward the kitchen. 'Maybe it's not such a good idea,' he whispered. 'While Jared's still on the loose, I mean.'

'The hell with Jared,' countered Ben. But secretly he was becoming increasingly convinced that this little picnic of theirs might just be the thing he needed to flush that bastard out. 'Don't you go postponin' it, now. I'll be there.'

'Well. . . .'

'Aw, come on, Conrad. It's been a busy day. Haven't I earned all that speechifyin' an' such?'

'That and more, Ben. I just—'

'That's settled, then,' Ben interrupted forcefully. 'You'll give me my watch, I'll give you my shield, we'll each say a few words an' that'll be an end to it.'

Kane showed him a pained smile. 'Well, I hope it'll have a little more dignity to it than that, but . . . all right,' he said with a sigh. 'All right, Ben. You win.'

His mind still on Jared, Ben told himself gravely, *For everyone's sake, I'd better.*

He tried to rest up, but anything more than an awkward doze was impossible. Eyes closed, he heard Doc and Frank let themselves out, and Nora wheel herself back into the parlour and, as he listened to the squeak her chair made, he thought some more about Jared, and how good it was going to feel to settle things with that sonofabitch once and for all.

Still, he cautioned himself against overconfidence. He was going to have the odds stacked against him if Jared *did* put in an appearance. For one thing, his gun-arm was as good as useless to him right now, so there was no point in wearing the Whitney to the picnic. Unarmed, then, and shot-up, he'd be Jared's for the taking.

But then again, maybe *not*.

'Ben?'

He opened his eyes.

'How are you feeling?' asked Nora, studying him with a frown.

'Like I been rode hard an' left out wet,' he said, and gave her a crooked smile.

She didn't return it. 'They didn't give you any

choice, did they?' she asked softly. 'Those men you killed?'

She wanted to know for certain that he hadn't deliberately gone looking for trouble, for that final blaze of glory, and he obliged her. 'Nope.' Then he sat forward carefully. 'That reminds me. Someone ought to go tell McGivern the good news. Reckon he'll rest a sight easier knowin' them fellers is finally off his tail.'

'That's what I'd like to see *you* do,' she remarked pointedly, wheeling herself backward so that he could squeeze past her. 'Rest.'

'Aw, I'll be fine. *Better* be. We still got that damn' picnic to attend, remember?'

She sat up a little straighter. 'You mean it's still on? I thought Conrad would have cancelled it, after all that's happened.'

'He wanted to,' Ben explained casually, 'but I'd as soon get the damn' thing over an' done with.'

'Are you sure you're up to it?'

'Uh-huh.'

Still feeling a little light-headed and trying not to let it show, he shuffled through the house to the bedroom, where he opened the door a crack and peered inside. McGivern was stretched out in the centre of the bed, his red-fair hair showing like a smear of blood against the whiteness of the pillow-case. Ben studied him briefly, the way his freckles stood out sharp against the paleness of his skin, and the occasional twitch of his near-white eyelashes, then turned to go, figuring to let him rest while he could and give him the news later.

'M-marshal. . . ?'

He turned back to find McGivern watching him through bloodshot, very blue eyes. 'Didn't mean to wake you,' he said, going inside.

McGivern pulled a face. 'You . . . didn't. I've been awake a while.'

'Doc says you're gonna be fine,' said Ben, coming to a halt at the foot of the bed.

'Well, I guess he ought to know,' McGivern allowed dreamily. And then, for the first time, he became aware of the sling in which Ben was carrying his right arm, and the bandage around his head. He said weakly, 'Wh-what the . . . hell happened to you?' And then, with sudden alarm, 'It wasn't—'

Ben said, 'Before you get your bowels in an uproar, McGivern – they're dead.'

Silence filled the room for a long moment as McGivern tried to make sense out of that. 'The Elliotts . . ?' he began.

Ben nodded. 'An' Patch Samuels, yeah. All dead.'

'What happened?'

Ben gave him the condensed version and then fell silent while the former Pinkerton man took it all in. A few moments later, he saw something liquid move in McGivern's morphine-glazed eyes, just before the man turned his face quickly toward the window. 'It's over, then,' McGivern croaked, as if he were almost afraid to believe it.

'It's over,' said Ben, and he added silently, *For you, at least*.

Turning back to face him, McGivern said thickly,

'What can I say, Marshal? "Thanks" . . . Hell, that doesn't even begin to cover it.'

'Ferget it,' Ben said gruffly. 'Jus' rest up an' get well. You're all right now, McGivern. Everythin's all right.'

And he thought, *Leastways, it will be once I've punched Jared's clock for him.*

A little after six o'clock there came a brisk rapping at the front door, and when Ben answered it, he found Kane standing in front of an open-topped Victoria coach, grinning like a fool and rubbing his hands in anticipation of the festivities to come.

'Are you folks all ready?' he asked in high good humour.

Ben heard Nora wheel herself up beside him. Her eyes were fixed on the elegant, slipper-shaped coach. 'Oh, Conrad!' she said admiringly.

Kane shrugged modestly, but it was obvious that he was pleased with her reaction. 'Nothing's too good for you today, Nora,' he said grandly. 'Nor for Ben, here.'

The day's muggy heat was finally starting to ease off at last, and the coming evening was shaping up to be agreeably cool. Nora had changed into a white blouse that buttoned tight to the throat and cuffs, and a full burgundy-coloured skirt. At her insistence, Ben, too, had made an effort, and between the two of them they'd gotten his old California pants off and a more presentable pair of pressed black trousers on. Because Nora had also made him wear a black string tie, he now looked self-conscious in the extreme.

'If you'll allow me . . .' said Kane, and he went around behind Nora and wheeled her out to the coach, then bent and lifted her into his arms. 'I hope your husband isn't the jealous type, ma'am,' he muttered jokingly as he lifted her into the vehicle.

'If he is,' she replied, matching his tone, 'he's certainly kept it well hidden all these years.'

As Ben followed them out and closed the door behind him, he carefully surveyed their surroundings from beneath the brim of his old black Stetson. The slowly setting sun was already bathing the town a deep, lustrous orange, and encouraging shadows to grow and deepen everywhere he looked, but of Jared there was no sign. Kane, meanwhile, was picking up Nora's chair and placing it carefully in back of the coach. 'You need any help climbing aboard, Ben?' he asked, a little breathlessly.

Ben shook his head. 'I can manage.' And, impulsively, he added, 'You're a good man, Conrad.'

Kane looked at him a little sidelong, surprised by the unexpected compliment. 'Why . . . thank you, Ben. I *do* try.'

When Ben and Nora were seated inside the coach, Kane climbed aboard, gathered the lines and put them on a course that would take them down towards First Street. Ben sat stiff and tense all the while, knowing that Jared could pick them off any time he chose. He made no attempt at conversation, just kept his eyes moving this way and that, looking for trouble, expecting it, *dreading* it.

At length they came out onto the southernmost tip of First Street, and Nora got her first look at all those banners and the garish red, white and blue bunting that marked the far northern end of town, and she murmured, with a choking kind of sound, 'Oh, Ben. . . .'

Ben only sighed uncomfortably and called, 'Pull up by the jailhouse for me, will you, Conrad? I better check on my prisoners while we're here.'

Kane called back over one shoulder, 'A lawman to the end, eh, Ben?'

'Yeah,' said Ben. 'Whatever.'

Kane drew the coach to a halt and Ben climbed down, still moving stiffly in order to favour his wounds. He unlocked the heavy oak door, went inside and reappeared again a few moments later. Kane asked him how Graham and Sutherland were doing, and he replied curtly, 'Still protestin' their innocence.'

Then he was back aboard and the coach was moving again, and beside him, Ben felt Nora tensing with excitement as the rows of cloth-covered trestle tables and the platform that reminded him so much of a gallows came ever closer. He felt like telling Kane to get this rig turned around and headed back to the peace and quiet of home, but held his silence and carried on looking from left to right and back again, his concerns still dominated by Jared, and what he stood to lose if this thing didn't pan out the way he hoped it would.

Up ahead, townsfolk were watching them come, and Ben, hating the attention, started feeling self-conscious all over again. He saw that five men who played a variety of instruments passably well had gathered together on the left-hand boardwalk. Now they struck up an enthusiastic rendition of 'For He's A Jolly Good Fellow'.

'Oh, Ben,' Nora said again, and she was so overcome by emotion that she could hardly make herself heard above the music.

Townsmen, women and their children started cheering, whistling and applauding them then. Hats were thrown in the air, and the horses pulling the coach started shying and side stepping a bit, unnerved by all the commotion. Entering into the spirit of the occasion, Nora started waving back at the congregation and Ben, feeling compelled to do *something*, at least, offered a few perfunctory nods. The tables, he saw, had been fairly loaded with food: puddings made from apples and breadcrumbs, cherry pies, stuffed turkey, hot rolls, squash, turnips, fried and mashed potatoes, bowls of steaming giblet gravy – and the sight and smell of it all reminded him that he still hadn't eaten anything since breakfast.

The clapping and cheering went on while Kane drew the coach to a halt in front of the platform and then hurried to lift Nora down into his arms. Ben climbed down too, starting to feel it himself now, God help him, this incredible wave of excitement, passion and warmth from the people he'd served all these years, and for the first time, he really began to understand and appreciate what they had done to honour him here this day.

He scanned the crowd, still nodding at them, still searching vainly for some sign of Jared, until he heard Kane call his name. Then he turned his head and saw that the mayor had carried Nora up onto the platform, where a special table of honour had been set, and was indicating that he should join them. He climbed the rough steps slowly, expecting a bullet in the back with every passing second, but reached the top in one piece and then, at Kane's enthusiastic urging, took the seat beside Nora, who was fairly glowing with pride.

Kane, meanwhile, faced the crowd and raised his hands for silence. 'Friends . . .' he called as the noise slowly faded to an expectant hush. 'Friends—'

But before he could say any more, he was distracted by a soft, burbling sound a short way to his left. He glanced sideways, at Ben, who made an expression of apology and rubbed meaningfully at his empty belly.

Smiling his understanding, Kane turned back to his audience and said smoothly, 'As you all know, we've gathered here this evening to pay tribute to Ben Crawford. And *paying* tribute is exactly what I intend to do to this man who has given so much of himself to the welfare of our little community. But you all know me, friends. I'm a politician at heart, and that means I like to keep people happy, especially *hungry* people. So . . . what say we eat first, and save what Ben would call my "speechifying", for later, huh?'

That won him another cheer, after which 'most everyone made a rush for the tables, where the hard-working ladies of the Church League, still clad in starched white aprons, went to work passing out plates and inviting folks to dig in.

Generous helpings of everything were brought up to Ben, Nora and Kane, and all at once the entire town was caught up in a happy, holiday mood. Empty as he was, however, Ben just toyed with his meal, too keyed-up to eat. He kept glancing around to check on their surroundings, unable to shake the feeling of being exposed and vulnerable, like he was being watched, like time was running out. . . .

The meal wore on. There was sarsaparilla for the children, a non-alcoholic punch for the women and apple cider for the men. Ben ignored his schooner, knowing it would be better to keep a clear head.

Nora, seeing how little he'd eaten, asked, 'Are you feeling all right, Ben?'

He nodded. 'Sure. Jus' got no stomach for this kind of affair, that's all.'

How long it went on, he couldn't say. It seemed like hours, but he doubted that it was even one. Then empty plates were shoved aside, belts were loosened a notch, children were told to go and play, and Kane finally climbed back to his feet.

'Here comes all that "speechifying" you've been waiting for,' he said, and good-natured laughter rippled through the assembly.

He paused then, for quite a while, as if organizing his thoughts. It was a trick he'd learned over the years, to make people sit up and take notice, and it certainly got their attention now. 'Ben Crawford's a modest man,' he went on at length, 'so I'll keep this short, in order to spare his blushes. But the simple facts are these.

'When I first sought him out twelve years ago, and asked him to come and make his life here in Kane's Crossing, I did so because I'd been told that Ben was one of the best town-tamers in the business, and that's what I wanted for our town – the best. But I soon discovered that I had been misinformed. Ben Crawford wasn't just *one* of the best – he was the *very* best. He came here and, by virtue of his reputation alone, kept the peace better than I ever expected, and we're all beholden to him for that.

'But I myself am even more in his debt than the rest of you, for not only did I hire us a first-rate lawman all those years ago . . . I also found myself a good and loyal friend.'

He fell silent again, and into the sudden quiet, men cleared their throats and women dabbed their eyes.

'Yes,' Kane continued. 'Ben made a fine job of keeping the peace, and when the town council decided that we no longer needed a marshal, that we could and should rely instead upon the territorial authorities, it was not a decision we took lightly. Ben warned us that New Mexico was still far from settled, but we dismissed his warning because we thought we knew better. We *didn't*.' He paused once more. 'I daresay you've all heard something about the trouble we've had in town today. Well, those events have shown us that we can never afford to be complacent where matters of law and order are concerned.'

A few men bobbed their heads and murmured their agreement. Ignoring them, Kane concluded, 'Our celebration here this evening was meant to mark the end of Ben's career as a lawman. But earlier this afternoon, I called an emergency meeting of the town council, and we agreed that it would be far better if we owned up to our mistake and asked Ben to stay on, full-time. If he says yes, then this gathering here today is not to celebrate his retirement, but rather to celebrate his first twelve years in office, and to look forward to the *next* twelve!'

Had someone built a roof over First Street, the cheer that greeted that announcement would have raised it for sure. The townsfolk went crazy again, cheering and clapping, whistling and throwing their hats in the air. Nora reached out and squeezed Ben's shoulder, and he started a little, because he was still thinking about Jared, and how that sonofabitch had better strike soon, else he'd miss his chance.

'Ben!' she husked. 'Ben, did you hear that?'

Kane turned to him and said, 'Well, Ben? What do you say?'

EIGHT

'Ben?' prompted the mayor.

Ben looked up at him, knowing he couldn't just sit there forever, that he must make some kind of response, and after another moment he climbed slowly to his feet. He could hardly hear himself think above all the cheering and whooping, and his headache, which had subsided to a dull throb, suddenly returned with a vengeance. He straightened to his full height, painfully aware that he was now giving Jared the best target he was ever likely to get, and all at once the anxiety in him reached a new pitch.

But nothing happened. There was no racketing gunblast, no sudden punch of hot, spinning lead, no screams, no eternal, black silence . . . and after one more tense moment, he released his pent-up breath in a slow, gusty sigh and thought, Face it, Jared's not gonna show. He's saving you for somethin' else.

Below him, the townsfolk fell silent again, waiting for him to say something, and he muttered halt-

ingly, 'I, ah ... I ain't much of a one for public
speakin', but ... well, I guess I should thank you
folks for ... everythin' you've done for me an' Nora,
here. Guess I ought to thank Conrad, too, for all
them fine things he said about me. I'm not sure that
I deserve 'em all, but ... well, he was right about
one thing: you folks live a good, peaceable life here-
abouts, but you shouldn't take it for granted. This
territory – the whole o' the South-west, iffen it
comes to that – it's still got a ways to go yet before it
can afford to do away with men the likes o' me.
Which, uh, brings me to that handsome offer Conrad
jus' made.'

He shuffled his feet awkwardly, wanting to get
it all said so that he could sit down again.
'Upholdin' the law ... well, that's jus' about all
I've ever done, or wanted to do. But we had some
trouble earlier today, three men with murder in
mind, an' I had to brace 'em. There was a fight, an'
they died ... an' to tell you the truth, I still don't
know why that was. By rights, it shoulda been *me*
that died, 'cause my mind was elsewhere most o'
the time we was tradin' shots. An' – you know
what I was thinkin'?'

He shook his head, as if in wonder. 'I was thinkin'
'bout Nora,' he said, and no one was more surprised
to hear that than Nora herself. ' 'Bout Nora, an' how
much I'd've given to be anyplace else than where I
was right then.'

Regret showed briefly in his blue eyes. 'I didn't
want to kill them boys,' he went on, 'nor have them

kill me. Right then, I didn't even want the responsibility that goes with this here shield no more. I jus' wanted to be at home, growin' old with my woman. So, that bein' the case, I got to thank you again, Conrad. I 'preciate what you're offerin' me . . . but I got to say no. Reckon I'll retire while I still got a few good years left in me.'

He looked at Kane, waiting for some kind of response. Around them, the town was absolutely silent. Then Kane smiled and stuck out his left hand, and as Ben took it and they shook, the five-piece band struck up another chorus of 'For He's A Jolly Good Fellow', the sombre mood lifted and the townsfolk started cheering themselves hoarse again.

'For what it's worth,' said Kane, having to raise his voice above the clamour, 'I think you made a wise decision, Ben.'

He reached into his suit jacket and brought out a small velvet box, from which he took a heavy, handsome gold Ingersoll watch and chain. Seeing it glitter in the slanting, early-evening sun, the crowd gradually fell silent again, knowing that here, at last, was the culmination of Crawford Day. Kane looked at Ben, opened his mouth to speak, decided that further speech was impossible for him right then, and shook his head. A moment later, he held the watch out and murmured thickly, 'On behalf of the people of Kane's Crossing, thank you for everything, Ben . . . and God bless you.'

Surprised by the strength of his own emotions,

Ben reached for the timepiece—
    —and that was when the damn' thing exploded.

For a moment no one properly knew what had
happened.

Then the deep, throaty roar of a long gun booming
along First Street told its own story. A .44.40 slug
had ripped the watch from Kane's hand and sent the
shattered pieces flying in all directions, and Ben,
knowing instantly who had fired the shot, suddenly
experienced a fierce, frightened kind of joy that the
waiting was finally over: that, for good or ill, the
time had finally come for this one last showdown.

Below him, in the street, confusion reigned as
women started screaming, or calling to their frightened children in high, panicky voices, and startled
men climbed to their feet and turned their heads
this way and that, searching for some sign of the
rifleman.

He wasn't difficult to spot.

A lone figure, moving with a distinctive mixture
of shuffle and limp, came hobbling down the centre
of First: a tall, half-starved man heading for thirty,
holding a still-smoking Winchester rifle in hands
that were unusually large and long-fingered.

Ben heard Kane whisper, 'Oh, God.'

Folks watched him come, frowned at him because
there was something strangely familiar about him,
and when at last they put a name to the face, and
that name rippled back through the crowd in a
series of hurried whispers, they drew back from

him, let him shuffle-limp past without challenge, and in his wake he left an awed kind of hush.

Up on the platform, Ben dared to tear his own gaze away from Jared just long enough to glance down at Nora. Her eyes were big and scared, her mouth a small, horrified *O*.

Then Jared was close enough for him to make out more detail: the way his shaggy, blue-black hair stuck out from beneath his sweat-marked grey hat, the pocked, whiskery face that was all cheekbones and buzzard-beak nose, and he swallowed hard, for this was more scarecrow than man, but a deadly dangerous scarecrow nonetheless.

Enjoying the fear he was inspiring in the people around him, Jared started climbing the steps to the platform, having to grab the crude handrail in order to drag himself ever higher. 'Marshal,' he greeted mockingly, his thin mouth forming a cold, impudent grin as the ice-chip eyes flickered briefly toward Nora. 'Miz Crawford.'

To one side and a little behind Ben now, Kane took a pace forward and said in a low voice, 'That's far enough—'

But Jared, just reaching the top step, fired the Winchester one-handed, and Kane cried out and buckled to his knees, bleeding from the right shoulder. Nora screamed, her scream joining those of all the other women and, as Kane hunched up and started sobbing, Jared only smiled the wider, for he'd made his point, and shown the rest of Kane's Crossing what they could expect if they should also be foolish enough to try and brace him.

Belly clenched tighter than ever, Ben fought the urge to turn and see what he could do for Kane. Kane, his breathing loud and shuddery now, would just have to wait. Instead, he and Jared traded stares, each man evaluating the other, seeing how the intervening years had marked him, until at length Ben said quietly, 'Been expectin' you, Jared.'

Jared's sneer flattened out. 'Thought you might, somehow.'

Ben inspected him some more, making no secret of it, showing no fear. 'Never thought you'd show yourself in these parts again,' he remarked, his tone mild. 'Want to tell me why you've come back?'

Jared pondered on that for a moment, then answered the question with one of his own. 'You got any idea what it's like in prison, Marshal?'

Ben hesitated. 'I know it isn't pretty,' he said at last.

Jared snorted at the understatement. 'Well, let me tell you,' he hissed, speaking between set teeth. 'For a feller who valued his freedom the way I did, a feller who'd never known anythin' but freedom, it was more like *hell!*'

He had the Winchester back in a steady two-handed grip now, with the barrel pointed dead-centre of Ben's belly, and as he spoke he levered a fresh shell into the breech. 'Open country, country as far as the eye could see,' he went on, 'that's what I was born to, Marshal. The land, the sky, the good, clean air .... never knowed anythin' different.

Never lived in a town, never wanted to, didn't want to be fenced in.' He snorted again, and spittle flecked the corners of his thin mouth. 'Freedom,' he snarled bitterly, 'that's what I had, what I *always* had . . . 'til they sent me to the Hardin County Pen, a'course. Then all I got was high walls an' barred windows, an' a cell not much bigger'n an outhouse.'

'You're lucky you didn't get a noose,' said Ben.

Jared gave him a strange, unsettling look. '*I* don't think so,' he muttered.

'What's that supposed to mean?'

'It means you never should've stopped 'em from hangin' me that night, Marshal. Iffen you'd let 'em string me up like they wanted to, I never would've had to spend six years dyin' a slower death inside that hell-hole.'

Ben narrowed his eyes. 'That's why you came back?' he asked in disbelief. 'Because I stopped a bunch of hot-heads from stretchin' your worthless neck?'

'Uh-huh.'

'Then you must be even crazier than I thought, you sorry-looking sonofabitch.'

Jared moved the barrel of the Winchester just a fraction, so that it was pointed at Nora. 'Careful now, Marshal,' he rasped. 'Nothin' crazy about a man payin' off an old debt.'

Ben said, 'You've got it all wrong, Jared. I'm the one who's owed. Me an' Nora.'

Jared shook his head some more. 'Because o' what you did that night,' he said, I ended up losin' the one thing I valued the most – my liberty.' His teeth showed briefly, and a crazy glow entered his deepset blue eyes. 'So I guess it's only right that you should lose the thing that means the most to *you*, too.'

Ben thought, a little desperately, Nora. He's gonna kill Nora. And he saw Jared's finger whiten around the Winchester's trigger.

But then—

'Jared.'

The voice, coming right out of the blue, made him flinch, made Jared stiffen, too. The barrel of the Winchester dropped an inch or so, and Jared turned a little, looked back over one shoulder, down toward the high double doorway of Mike O'Driscoll's livery stable.

He said, like he couldn't believe it, '*Pa?*'

Elmer Parsons came walking out of the shadows, his old Brown Manufacturing breech-loader held across his narrow chest, and Ben saw that the tall, skinny rancher had taken his advice, cleaned himself up, had come to pay his respects – but had come loaded for bear, too.

Elmer slowed to a halt at the foot of the steps, not once taking his sad blue eyes off the son he feared so much, and had come to hate because of it. 'I had a notion you'd show up here tonight,' he said, his voice resigned and lifeless.

Jared gave him a hard, sideways look. 'Well, you was right,' he muttered. 'Now put up that damn' rifle an' make dust.'

Elmer's rubbery lips pursed. 'Turn a blind eye so's

you can keep on killin'?' he asked. 'Naw. One more killin', Jared – an' then it stops for good.'

Emotion made his face twist all out of shape then and, clumsily, he brought the ancient rifle up. But Jared was way ahead of him. He started twisting all the way around, his Winchester moving with him, the barrel dipping towards his father – and that was when Ben made his move.

He bawled, '*Jared*!'

Something in the savagery of it made Jared turn back to him, just as Ben's left hand blurred sideways, into the sling which was cradling his right arm. Three, four seconds passed, and then Ben brought the hand back out, folded around the tiny weapon he'd retrieved from his office shortly before the picnic – Arthur Jameson's Remington double derringer.

Jared's eyes went wide, his mouth dropped open, he started dragging himself back around—

Ben shot him twice in the face.

The force of the small-calibre bullets pushed Jared backwards on legs like jelly, and then he started falling tail-over-tip down the rough steps, his face a red mess, the rifle clattering from his lifeless fingers.

Moments later he came to rest at Elmer's feet.

Ben sagged then, and let the derringer fall from his trembling hand. He looked at Nora, dropped to a crouch beside her and buried his face in the dip between her neck and shoulder. 'Are you all right?' he asked urgently. 'Are—'

She reached out to cradle him gently. 'I'm all right, Ben,' she whispered shakily. 'I'm . . . all right.'

He wanted to hold her and go on holding her, but Kane needed his help, too. He squeezed her hand, then broke away from her and turned to the ashen-faced mayor, who was sprawled on his back on the far side of the platform, a bloodstain spreading across his right sleeve. 'Hold still a minute, Conrad,' he muttered. 'Let's take a look at you. . . .'

'*I'll* do that,' said Doc Warren, clumping across the platform to kneel beside the mayor.

While Doc did exactly that, Ben glanced over one shoulder. Now that Jared was dead, whatever spell he'd cast over Kane's Crossing had been broken, and most of the townsfolk were crowding forward, deter-mined to lend a hand.

'Ben,' wheezed Kane, bringing his head back around. 'I thought . . . I thought we were all done for. . . .'

'Easy, now,' said Doc, cutting the sleeve of Kane's jacket so that he could inspect the wound more clearly.

'Not you, though,' Kane continued in a gasp. 'By God, Ben, I wasn't exaggerating, was I? You really *are* the best in the business. F. . .full of surprises.'

Ben shrugged carefully. He didn't really know what to say to that, so all he said, stupidly, was, 'A good lawman always keeps a little somethin' up his sleeve.'

Kane tried to laugh, but it came out more like a sob, and Ben threw an anxious glance at Doc, who said calmly, 'Don't worry. He'll be fine.'

Leaving Doc to it, he climbed unsteadily to his feet and turned back to Nora just as Elmer Parsons led a ribby sorrel horse out of the stable, tucked his unused rifle into a worn sheath strapped to the saddle, and mounted up. He called, '*Elmer*!'

But if Elmer Parsons heard him, he gave no sign, just walked the horse slowly northward, into the growing dusk, looking neither left nor right.

He made to yell Elmer's name again, then stopped. What could he say that Elmer would want to hear right then? That he was sorry? He wasn't. He shook his head, wanting to do something to ease Elmer's pain but not knowing what.

And then he felt Nora's hand on his good arm, and looked down at her. 'Leave him, Ben,' she said softly. 'Tomorrow's another day.'

And he knew she was right. Tomorrow *was* another day, the first day of his retirement. And perhaps in the free days and weeks and months ahead, he and Nora would spend some time out at the Parsons place, helping Elmer to start living again.

The idea appealed to him.

He reached up, unpinned the shield from his shirt-front, and slowly, carefully, set it down on the table in front of him. Then, taking Nora's hand in his, he said gently, 'Come on, little darlin'. Let's go home.'